DANNY MANN
SUPER FAN

Ian Slatter

ianslatter.com
@slatter_ian

Copyright

DANNY MANN SUPER FAN

First edition. May 2021.

Written by Ian Slatter.

ISBN: 9798572669824

Chapter 1

'How long's left?' asked Danny.

'Five minutes,' answered his dad, 'plus whatever they add on for injury time.'

'Five minutes!? We'll never hold on that long.'

'We might Danny, we might,' said Danny's gran.

'Keep the faith son, keep the faith,' Dad told him.

That was easier said than done, thought Danny, after the season Chadmouth Town had had. He'd lost count of the number of late goals they'd conceded to throw away a win or a draw. If football matches were all 80 minutes long instead of 90 they'd probably be on course for promotion instead of being bottom of the table and facing relegation.

'How long now?'

'Four minutes.'

It was unbearable. Chadmouth desperately needed a win and three valuable points, but when they were only 1-0 up and the other team was throwing everything they had at them, the points were far from safe. Danny could barely watch.

'How long...'

'For goodness sake, Danny, stop asking me how long's left,' Dad snapped. 'You shouldn't have forgotten your phone, then you wouldn't need to keep asking me.' Danny was nervous, and he wasn't helping anyone else's nerves either.

He stood up and shouted as loud as he could, 'Come on you Crabs!'

Chadmouth was a town that was once a small fishing village, and there was a crab on their football team's badge in honour of that, giving them their nickname the Crabs. Danny sat back down and fought the urge to ask his dad again how much longer was left.

Then, their opponents, Burbank Rovers, won a corner. This was it, thought Danny. Their defence was *bound* to leave someone completely unmarked to head it straight into the net. The corner came in, it was half-cleared, the ball was hit back in and it struck the post. A defender tried to scramble it away but it hit his teammate. The crowd oohed and aahed. There was a shot but it was blocked. The goalie tried to grab it but missed. Someone else tried to shoot, the ball struck a boot and flew up into the air, and hit someone's hand. The ref blew his whistle. What had he given? A penalty!

'No!' shouted Danny.

'No!' shouted Dad and Gran.

'No!' shouted everyone in the crowd, apart from the visiting fans, who were jumping up and down and cheering wildly.

'How is that a penalty?'

'It just hit his hand, he didn't know anything about it.'

'It hit one of their players, not ours.'

The ref couldn't hear them though, not that it would have made any difference if he could.

'They might miss the penalty,' said Gran, hopefully.

Burbank's striker, who Danny knew was their top scorer, placed the ball on the penalty spot. A big man who for some reason always took his shirt off to watch the game, even when it was freezing, looked like he was praying for a miracle. Chadmouth's goalie, Mortensen, waved his arms around and jumped about on the goal-line, trying to put his opponent off. Danny was sat right on the edge of his blue, plastic seat. He wanted to look the other way, but he couldn't *not* watch. The penalty-taker stepped up, struck the ball... and sent it flying into the top corner of the net.

All the crowd groaned, apart from the away fans, who somehow managed to be even more excited than when they'd won the penalty. Some of the Chadmouth fans started to leave the stadium. They'd seen enough.

'1-1 isn't the end of the world. At least it's a point,' said Dad.

'A point could make all the difference at the end of the season,' nodded Gran.

Danny knew they were just trying to put a brave face on it though. They desperately needed to be picking up three points for a win now, not just one for a draw. Besides, it wasn't over yet. They might not even get a point.

Right on cue, the fourth official put up his electronic board to show that there would be six minutes of injury time. Another groan went around the Springly Park ground.

'Six minutes?! Where has he got six minutes from?'

Chapter 2

Danny just knew exactly what would happen, as did the rest of the Chadmouth supporters, and sure enough, four minutes later Burbank sent a long ball forward. It should have been easy for the defender, Sagar, to boot it clear, as there was nobody else anywhere near him, but disaster struck. He slipped as he tried to turn to clear it, and the Burbank striker, brimming with confidence after scoring the penalty, ran through and controlled the loose ball. He raced through on goal. Mortensen came out to challenge him, but the Burbank man neatly chipped the ball over his head. It bounced once, twice, then nestled in the back of the net.

And that was that. Chadmouth had about a minute after the restart to equalise, but never looked like doing so, and the final whistle soon rang out to seal their defeat. *Another* defeat. They'd had far too many this season, and it was looking more and more likely that they were going to be relegated. The away fans were cruelly reminding them of this as the crowd started for the exits, chanting 'Going down, going down, going down!' A few Chadmouth fans were shouting for the manager to be sacked, but he'd only been given the job about a month ago after their last boss was given the boot, so that was unlikely to happen.

Danny was close to tears as they slowly left their seats. It was so unfair. A dodgy penalty decision and an unfortunate slip had cost them the match, and that sort of thing had been happening over and over again all season.

They exited the stadium and started slowly walking home. The narrow, terraced streets were crowded at first, but they quickly thinned out as they got further from the ground. Officially it was called the Doh-Ray-Me-Far Solar Panel Arena, after the club had signed a sponsorship deal with a local business, but everyone still called it Springly Park, its original name.

They lived about a mile from the ground, but that was quite a long walk for Gran these days. She'd been going since she was younger than Danny, and he often wondered just how many times she'd walked to and from Springly Park. He also wondered today how many times she'd seen her team throw away a lead over the years. To Danny it felt like it happened every single week, either because of their poor play or because of bad luck.

'We must be the unluckiest football team in the world,' said Gran, as if reading his mind.

'You make your own luck,' said Dad, wheeling out one of the football commentators' favourite clichés. 'It evens itself out over the season,' he added, throwing in another old football saying for good measure.

'I don't think it does,' Danny disagreed.

'We're not down yet,' said Gran, trying to look on the bright side as always.

'We pretty much are.' Danny wasn't as positive as his Gran was.

'It's not all over 'til the fat lady sings,' she told him.

'Hah! I think I heard her warming up when that goal went in at the end,' laughed Dad.

Gran had a chuckle at that as well. How could either of them be laughing? Danny felt like he wouldn't even be able to smile until at least the middle of next week.

He wasn't sure how much more he could take. It was depressing, turning up every Saturday afternoon, desperately hoping that something would change, only to have his hopes dashed and seeing his team lose once again. Did even want to go again next week? He didn't think he could face it.

It really was looking grim for the Crabs. That defeat had left them rooted to the bottom of the table, nine points from safety with eight games to go. Winning enough points to overtake four of the teams above them to avoid getting relegated to League Two was a tough task, and right then he had very little hope that they'd manage it.

Danny knew though, deep inside, that by Friday he'd have somehow got his hopes back up. He'd have convinced himself that there was some reason why their form was about to pick up and that they could still pull off a great escape. He'd be there on Saturday, cheering them on, whatever happened. That's what being a real fan was all about. You stuck with your team through thick and thin.

They really could do with a bit of luck though.

Beddingley City 2-1 Libley United
Chadmouth Town 1-2 Burbank Rovers
Kenton Athletic 2-2 Plumborough Town
Northford 0-1 Marshfield County
Stimport Rangers 0-0 Finbury Rovers

		Played	Won	Drawn	Lost	GD	Points
19	Finbury	38	10	7	21	-19	37
20	Beddingley	38	8	11	19	-13	35
21	Plumborough	38	6	13	19	-28	31
22	Kenton	38	6	11	21	-28	29
23	Marshfield	38	5	12	21	-31	27
24	Chadmouth	38	5	11	22	-35	26

Chapter 3

'Here he is!' shouted Ashton, as soon as Danny walked through the school gates. 'It's Danny Mann, Pants Team Fan!'

It was non-uniform day. Danny loved non-uniform day, but he hated it too. He loved the fact that (obviously) you didn't have to wear school uniform. Instead, he could wear, and he always did, his beloved red and blue hooped Chadmouth Town shirt, but that was where the problems always started. The instant the other kids saw it, the abuse would begin, and today was no different.

'What division are you in now – League Ten?' sneered Louis.

'League Twenty!' laughed Taylor.

'League One, *actually*,' said Danny crossly.

'League Hundred and One more like!'

'You're gonna be in League Two soon anyway - you're getting relegated,' Jackson told him.

'We haven't been relegated yet.'

'Yeah, whatever. You keep telling yourself that.'

'You don't deserve to be in *any* league, you're so rubbish.'

'What would any of *you* know about football anyway?' Danny shouted back, his face red with anger. 'None of you are real fans. You're all plastic fans.'

'Shut up Mann,' Ashton told him. 'You know nothing about football.'

'All *you've* done is pick a team you think's gonna win stuff,' Danny yelled back at him, 'then you say you support them, but you never go to their matches, you don't know what it *really* feels like when the team you love wins or loses. You don't *really* care. You'd probably pick a new team to support if the team you were pretending to support got relegated. Glory hunters!'

'Yeah? So what's the point in supporting a team that's so rubbish it never wins? Only an idiot would choose to do that.'

He had considered not wearing a Chadmouth shirt today, but that would just have attracted even more attention. He'd have been asked all day if he'd finally stopped supporting them and was going to support a "proper" team now, and why was he such a rubbish fan to give up on his team (even though that's what they were always telling him to do). So there was nothing to be gained by not wearing it, and anyway, he was proud of his team, even if they weren't doing very well at the moment. Nobody was going to stop him from wearing the red and blue Chadmouth Town colours.

Most of the other kids at his school supported the big Premier League teams - Liverpool, Manchester United, Manchester City, Arsenal, Chelsea – and he always thought of them as the Premier League Gang, or the Prem Gang for short. Some even supported the big Spanish sides like Real Madrid and Barcelona. Danny thought it was rubbish that none of them supported their local team, but they all just laughed whenever he said so.

The bell went, and Ashton and the others headed into school, still laughing and being rude about Chadmouth Town.

'Loser!' called Taylor over her shoulder, making an L on her forehead with her finger and thumb.

Danny started after them, but a hand on his arm held him back.

'Just try to ignore them,' said a boy wearing an England shirt.

Nelson was Danny's best friend. He was actually a Liverpool supporter, but he usually chose not to wear a Liverpool shirt whenever Danny was around so it didn't cause any arguments. Danny didn't have a problem with Nelson supporting Liverpool anyway, partly because Nelson didn't tease him about Chadmouth and partly because he had a good reason to support them. His dad had moved to Liverpool from Jamaica when he was a boy and was a lifelong Reds fan, who took great delight in telling Danny all about how he'd been there when Liverpool had famously come from three goals down to beat AC Milan to win the Champions League. He had taken Nelson to see Liverpool play at their ground, Anfield, for the first time when Nelson was just four. There was only one team Nelson was ever going to support, unlike the others, who Danny was sure had all just chosen the best teams in Europe, who were winning cups and league titles regularly and were able to pay big money for the world's best players. They knew nothing about *real* football as far as Danny was concerned.

Chapter 4

Danny and Nelson waited until most of the other kids had gone in before they went inside. The insults would continue throughout the day, but the less time they spent with the others, the fewer there would be.

The rest of the morning was pretty uneventful, with a boring assembly then a maths lesson, but then it was break-time. Everyone in their class, apart from some of the girls and Mikey, who preferred to run around the many lines painted on the concrete playground pretending to be a train, usually had a kick-about if someone had remembered to bring a ball in. Jackson had brought one in today, and they quickly picked teams and started a match. Danny could never resist a game of football, even if it meant playing with the Prem Gang.

It didn't take long for them to start picking on Danny again though. Every kind of mistake by anyone - shooting wide, a bad pass or missing the ball completely – was followed by shouts of 'Arrgghhh! Chadmouth!' and chants of 'You're worse than Chadmouth Town!'

Danny did his best to ignore them, but eventually he lost his temper. The ball fell to Ashton, who controlled it and started running towards goal. Danny went to challenge for the ball.

'And it's Ashton, to score the goal that sends Chadmouth Town down!' yelled Ashton as he lined up a shot.

Danny sprinted over to him and, instead of trying to tackle him or block the shot, just barged straight into him, sending him flying. Ashton landed heavily and looked for a second like he was going to cry, before he realised that everyone was watching him. The rest of the gang raced over to get involved, helping Ashton up and shoving Danny.

'What did you do that for?' demanded Ashton as he was helped up.

'Dirty Chadmouth filth,' snarled Louis.

Nelson arrived on the scene and started to pull Danny away from the crowd, but Ashton was back on his feet now and looking for revenge.

'Think you're hard do you?' he shouted in Danny's face. 'I'm gonna have you for that.'

Fortunately, Mrs Kaur, who was on playground duty, had spotted that there was a problem and came running up to calm things down.

'Stop that right now Ashton,' she called as she got there.

'It wasn't his fault Miss,' Taylor told her.

'That's right Miss,' agreed Jackson. 'It's Danny Mann's fault. He deliberately fouled Ashton. He did it on purpose.'

'He did Miss. We all saw him,' chipped in Louis.

'Is that right Danny?' asked Mrs Kaur.

Danny was beyond caring by now.

'Yeah,' he admitted, staring at the floor.

'Then you can go straight to Mr Quibley's office and tell him all about it,' Mrs Kaur told him. 'Go on. Straight away please.'

'I'll come with you,' offered Nelson, but Mrs Kaur stopped him.

'Danny's quite capable of going to Mr Quibley's office on his own thank you, Nelson.'

As Danny started to trudge back inside, Mrs Kaur spotted the ball lying, temporarily forgotten, at the side of the crowd, and snatched it up.

'I'll have this I think,' she announced.

'Aww, Miss…' started Jackson.

'Football has caused quite enough trouble for one day thank you very much. You can have it back at the end of the day,' she said, striding back towards the spot at the edge of the playground where the teachers liked to stand so they could see everything that was going on.

'Nice one Mann,' muttered Ashton.

'Yeah. Ruin it for everyone why don't you?' said Taylor.

'Crabby loser,' added Louis.

Chapter 5

'Oh dear, oh dear,' said Mr Quibley, with a sigh. 'Maybe I should have banned football shirts on non-uniform days like Mrs Kaur said I should.'

He'd only been the Head of Lemonbrook Primary School since the start of the school year, and this was the first non-uniform day since he'd taken over.

'They did tell me it causes nothing but trouble, but I insisted it would be fine. There we go. Lesson learned Mr Quibley. Always listen to your teaching staff.'

Danny tried not to smile. It was obvious why Mr Quibley had resisted calls to ban football shirts, as he sat behind his desk wearing a Chadmouth Town polo shirt, with a framed, signed Chadmouth Town shirt on the wall behind him. It was well known that he was a lifelong Crabs supporter and a regular at home matches, although Danny had never seen him there.

'Sorry Sir,' said Danny, feeling like he needed to say something.

'It's a shame, it really is,' continued Mr Quibley, as if he hadn't heard Danny. 'I'm all for a bit of banter, but why, oh why can it not just stop there?'

'Sorry Sir,' said Danny again, not knowing what else to say.

'I thought we'd seen the last of this sort of hooliganism, but no, it seems it's alive and kicking, literally, at Lemonbrook Primary.'

'I didn't kick him, Sir, I just…'

'I won't have it, Danny Mann, I won't have it. It won't do at all.'

'I'm sorry Sir, it's just… he'd been winding me up all day and I…'

'Danny, listen to me. One thing you can guarantee as a football fan, maybe the *only* thing you can guarantee, is that sooner or later someone else is going to have a go at you and your team. Even I'm not immune to it, you know.'

'You Sir?'

'Yes Sir, me Sir. Unfortunately for me, my wife's a massive Libley United fan, and she gave me grief for *weeks* after they thrashed us at the beginning of the season.'

'Oh yeah, that was a dreadful performance, I don't know why we…'

'My point is, I just had to take it didn't I? I didn't like it much, but it didn't stop me from loving my wife. And, I'd have done exactly the same to her if we'd stuffed them. It's just the way it is as a football fan. You can't go around physically attacking anyone who has a go at your team, no matter how much you want to. Do you understand?'

'Yes Sir.'

'You'll have to stay inside every break time and lunchtime for the rest of the week. Alright?'

'It's Friday today Sir,' Danny told him, then immediately wished he hadn't.

'Is it? Is it indeed? Well then, you can stay in all of next week as well. Understand?'

'Yes Sir,' Danny nodded. He knew his punishment could have been worse.

'And if this happens again I'm going to have to contact your parents and suggest that a break from attending matches might be a good idea.'

That would be a lot worse.

'It won't happen again Sir,' said Danny hurriedly. There was no way he was going to miss any matches.

He got up to leave the Head's office, as Mr Quibley returned to his paperwork.

'Could do with a win against Stimport tomorrow,' said Mr Quibley, without looking up, just before Danny closed the door.

'Yes Sir, definitely,' Danny agreed.

Mr Quibley carried on with his work, and Danny shut the door behind him.

* * *

When Danny got back to his class he ignored the sniggers from the Prem Gang and took his seat.

'Ah, Danny. Glad you could join us,' said his teacher, Miss Caper. 'There's a book on your desk. Please open it to chapter six and start reading.'

Danny sat down and did as he was told.

'In silence please!' added Miss Caper as a few whispered conversations started up around the classroom.

Danny felt thoroughly miserable. Constant teasing about Chadmouth Town, no break-times for a week and now he was having to read a totally boring book about, he realised after a couple of lines, some native American tribe who did some stupid dance to try to make it rain. He really wasn't in the mood to be reading about anything, let alone stupid, boring tribal dances. Although, if someone could do one now and make it pour with rain for the next week, he wouldn't be missing out on break-times, as everyone else would be stuck inside too. It was all mumbo-jumbo as far as he was concerned though, so he wasn't about to give it a try.

He started skim-reading, hoping he'd remember just about enough to answer if Miss decided to ask him a question. His thoughts soon turned though to Stimport Rangers, Chadmouth's next opponents, and he started making notes in his exercise book about the team selection and tactics he'd use to earn his team a much-needed win if he was their manager.

Chapter 6

It was Saturday morning again. Usually, Gran came round mid-morning whenever Chadmouth were at home, ready to have lunch before the three of them headed off to Springly Park, but Dad had told Danny that she wasn't feeling very well so wouldn't be going with them. It would be the first home match any of them had missed all season.

So that her season ticket didn't go to waste Dad had told Danny he could ask a friend along to take her place, and he'd had no hesitation in asking Nelson. There was no one else he'd wanted to ask, and no one else would have come anyway. Nelson had been up for it straight away, and his parents had said he could go. He wasn't a Chadmouth supporter, but he loved football and was happy to watch any match, anywhere.

Nelson arrived at Danny's house just as he was putting his Weetabixy bowl in the dishwasher. It was sunny, so they decided to go for a kickabout at the field nearby. They got Danny's ball out of the shed and headed down Fish Street and Blackberry Lane to get to the field, squeezing between some scruffy bushes and down a bank to get to the flat grassy area that many of the local kids used as a football pitch.

Danny found an old trainer with the sole falling off that someone had abandoned, and Nelson got a stick out of the bushes, and they used them for goal-posts. Nelson went in goal first and Danny started taking shots at him before they swapped round. In his head, Danny was playing up front for the Crabs at Springly Park, the top of which you could just see through the trees.

After about ten minutes they decided to take a break and sat down on the grass together.

'So, do you reckon Chadmouth will win today?' asked Nelson.

Danny sighed. 'I dunno. We've got to, sooner or later. We just need a bit of luck to win one, then we could go on a bit of a run perhaps.'

'If only you could control luck.'

'Um, it wouldn't be luck then, would it?'

'I suppose not. But what if you could control it though.'

'Yeah.'

'Like those native Americans we were reading about at school.'

'What?'

'They were trying to control the rain with their rain dance weren't they?'

'Oh yeah. I doubt it ever worked for them though.'

'Doesn't matter. It's worth a try.'

'What is?'

'A rain dance. I mean, a luck dance.'

'A luck dance?'

'Yeah, why not? Right. First of all, what we need is some sort of chant.'

'A chant?'

'Yeah. In the book it said they did a dance *and* a chant.'

'Okay. Do you know any chants?'

'Um, no. Don't you sing any at Chadmouth?'

'Well, there are some, but Dad's made me promise not to sing most of them.'

'Oh, right. I know some Liverpool ones, but that wouldn't be right would it? Hang on… I know. We learned one to sing around the campfire at Cub camp back in the summer.'

'Okay. Can you remember how it goes?'

'I think so. Right, repeat after me: Fi.'

'Fi.'

'Fi fie.'

'Fi fie.'

'Fi fie fo.'

'Fi fie fo.'

'Kumala.'

'Kumala.'

'Vista.'

'Vista.'

'Kumala kumala kumala vista.'

'Kumala kumala kumala vista.'

'Oh la-noh la-noh la-vista.'

'What the..? Do we really have to…'

'Just say it.'

'Okay, Okay. Oh la-noh la-noh la-vista.'

'Eenie meenie dessameenie ooh-aah ooh-orrameenie.'

'Eenie meenie dessameenie ooh-aah… what was it?'

'Eenie meenie dessameenie ooh-aah ooh-orrameenie.'

'Eenie meenie dessameenie ooh-aah ooh-orrameenie?'

'That's it. Beep deedly oden boden bodash skadutendaten.'

'What?!'

'Beep deedly.'

'Beep deedly.'

'Oden boden.'

'Oden boden.'

'Bodash skadutendaten.'

'Bodash skadutendaten.'

'Beep deedly oden boden bodash skadutendaten.'

'Beep deedly oden boden bodash skadutendaten.'

'There you go.'

'Wow. Who made that up?'

'I dunno. Some bloke at Cubs I guess.'

'And you think this is somehow going to make Chadmouth Town win today?'

'No. Yes. Maybe. It's worth a try, isn't it? What have we got to lose?'

'I guess.'

'Come on then. We just need some moves now.'

'Moves?'

'Yes, moves. It's not a dance without moves is it?'

Danny looked around to make sure there was nobody watching them, but the field was deserted apart from them.

'Okay. What have you got in mind?' he asked.

'Come on Danny. You've got to do some of the work here,' Nelson said. 'I did the chant, you can do the moves. It's for your team, remember.'

Chapter 7

Danny shook his head. He was starting to regret inviting Nelson now. He never had to come up with any dance moves when he went to the football with Gran.

'Alright then, how about this?' he began, walking round in a circle with long strides, punching the air in front of him and kicking out a leg to the side with each step.

'That's a start, but we need more,' said Nelson, falling in behind Danny and copying him.

'Okay, how about this?' said Danny, pulling his Chadmouth shirt up over his head.

'More, we still need more,' said Nelson, pulling his t-shirt up over his head as well.

Danny bent down to pick up the old trainer they'd been using as a goal-post. He looked around for something else and spotted an old, broken umbrella under a bush nearby. He went to get it, then held them both up to show Nelson, and raised them up in turn in time with his strides. Nelson laughed, then looked around for his own props, picking up the stick that had been the other goal-post. Then he spotted a black dog-poo bag that a dog owner had for some reason chucked on the ground after picking up their dog's stinky deposits.

'Nelson, that's disgusting' Danny cried with a grin, as Nelson picked it up on the end of his stick, which had a handy V shape in the end that could have been purpose-made for the task.

'Don't worry. I'll be careful. Now we need to add the chant,' said Nelson, and he started the chant they'd just practised as they strode round and round with their t-shirts over their heads and waving the smelly old trainer, broken brolly and stick with a bag of poo on the end.

'Fi.'

'Fi.'

'Fi fie.'

'Fi fie.'

'Fi fie fo.'

'Fi fie fo.'

'Kumala.'

'Kumala.'

'Vista.'

'Vista.'

'Kumala kumala kumala vista.'

'Kumala kumala kumala vista.'

'Oh la-noh la-noh la-vista.'

'Oh la-noh la-noh la-vista.'

'Eenie meenie dessameenie ooh-aah ooh-orrameenie.'

'Eenie meenie dessameenie ooh-aah ooh-orrameenie.'

'Beep deedly oden boden bodash skadutendaten.'

'Beep deedly oden boden bodash skadutendaten.'

They were in floods of tears now as they realised how stupid they looked and sounded, and they fell to the ground laughing. Fortunately, there was still nobody else there to see them.

'Right,' said Nelson when he'd got his breath back. 'Big finish.'

'Okay, what now?'

'On your knees, like this.'

Nelson got up on his knees, and Danny followed suit. They raised the stick with poo-bag, trainer and brolly to the skies.

'We call on you, the gods of football…'

'The gods of football?'

'Yeah, just go with it. We call on you, the gods of football, in exchange for this broken umbrella, old trainer and dog-poo bag on a stick. We call on you to give Chadmouth Town a bit of luck…'

'A lot of luck.'

'A lot of luck this afternoon, oh… um, gods.'

'Please.'

'If you don't mind.'

The boys started laughing again, until suddenly there was a crack of thunder from out of nowhere, and it started to rain.

'Oh no,' laughed Nelson. 'We haven't done a luck dance, we've accidentally done a rain dance!'

The rain started to fall more heavily, and they grabbed the ball and started running for home. The sun was still shining though, and a rainbow shone right over Springly Park. Danny wondered whether maybe, just maybe, they had managed to help Chadmouth Town.

Chapter 8

'Come on then lads,' said Dad as Danny and Nelson were finishing their cheese rolls with a side order of pickled onion Monster Munch, which Danny had told his mum was definitely one of his five-a-day as it had onion in it when she'd tried to get them to eat some salad. 'Time to go.'

They quickly scoffed the last of their lunch and pulled their trainers back on.

'You'd better wear coats,' Dad said, as he usually did, regardless of the weather.

'Nah,' said Danny. 'It's not cold.' The sudden rainstorm had stopped now, and it was sunny again.

'It'll be colder in the ground,' Dad warned.

'We'll be fine,' said Danny.

Danny and Dad checked they had their season ticket cards, and Dad gave Gran's to Nelson. Then, grabbing his keys as he went, Dad led the way out of the house, down the drive and up the road towards Springly Park.

There were a couple of routes they could take to the ground, which both took about the same time. Today they went along Station Road, then turned right onto Hope Street.

'Today's the day then, Danny,' announced Dad, with a hopeful look on his face.

'Today's the day what?' asked Danny.

'Today's the day when our luck turns. Three points today I reckon, then we're in with half a chance of staying up. What do you reckon Nelson?'

Nelson and Danny exchanged a quick glance.

'Uh, yeah, why not?' answered Nelson.

'We've never lost when you've been with us Nelson, have we, Danny?'

'He's only ever come with us once before,' said Danny.

'Yeah, and, as I recall, we drew didn't we?'

'Yeah,' agreed Danny. 'A boring nil-nil.'

'Like I said, we've never lost when Nelson's been with us.'

'Not sure you can read too much into that Dad.'

Dad shrugged.

'And besides,' Danny continued, 'we need more than a point today.'

'True.'

They turned left at the end of Hope Street, onto Harbour Road, then right onto Short Street. They were getting near the ground now, and other Chadmouth fans wearing red and blue shirts, and clutching flags and banners had joined them, all heading the same direction or standing around, waiting for mates at pre-arranged meeting points. Loud laughter was coming out of the pub next to the ground where lots of the fans went on match days. A man was selling Chadmouth Town scarves, hats and badges out of a shopping trolley, and the smell of fried onions started to reach their noses, wafting along from the hot-dog stall near the main entrance.

They reached the entrance and walked past a couple of police officers who were keeping a careful eye on everyone, making Danny think about what Mr Quibley had told him about football hooligans. Everyone was in a good mood and behaving themselves today though. Just outside the turnstiles, they stopped to buy a programme from a lady wearing a Chadmouth Town bobble hat, standing in a small booth with an "Official Programme" sign on it. Danny recognised her. She was always there, selling her programmes.

'Three points today?' she asked them as she handed Dad his change.

'Can't settle for anything less,' Dad told her, dropping his money back in his pocket.

They scanned their season ticket cards and entered the stadium. It was an old-fashioned ground that had seen better days if Chadmouth fans were honest, but it still held a very special place in their hearts and Danny wouldn't change a thing about it. It was his favourite place in the world. There were still twenty minutes before kick-off, so they were in no rush to get to their seats.

'Anyone need the toilet?' Dad asked. Danny wondered whether dads were trained to ask their kids if they needed the toilet whenever they were close to one. It seemed to be something they all did.

'Think I do,' said Nelson, wandering off towards the gents.

'I'm fine,' said Danny, staying where he was.

Nelson was back with them a few minutes later, and the three of them walked up the steps to their seats. The stadium announcer was reading out some dedications to supporters in the ground, mainly elderly fans whose birthday it was and kids attending their first ever match, and Nippy the Crab, Chadmouth Town's giant mascot, was making his way around the outside of the pitch waving to kids (and adults) in the stands.

'Shame you've been before,' Danny told Nelson. 'We could have got your name read out.'

'Yeah, shame,' said Nelson, although he didn't sound too disappointed. 'And *you* could have gone down to the front to fist-bump Nippy.'

'Claw bump,' Danny corrected him.

'Now, a reminder of your teams for today,' said the announcer excitedly over the tinny tannoy, running through first the home players then the visitors.

'Keenor – we used to have a player called Keenor didn't we?' said one of the men who always sat behind Danny and his dad as the away team was read out. 'Old Crusher Keenor? Played up front, back in the 70s.'

'No, you're thinking of Crusher Curtis, our centre back from the 80s.'

'Curtis wasn't called Crusher you old fool. He was Kicker – Kicker Curtis.'

'Kicker? We've never had anyone play for us called Kicker.'

'Yes we bloomin' well did. Kicker Curtis. Used to kick the opposition more than the ball. Sent off every other week.'

'That was Early-Bath Irving you numpty.'

Danny chuckled to himself as they continued to bicker. They found something to disagree about at least once every match, but they both seemed to enjoy it. Everyone enjoyed the match in their own, different way he supposed.

'Teams will be out in a minute,' said Dad, passing the programme to Danny to have a look at. Nelson busied himself on his phone, checking the Liverpool line-up for their Premier League match against Tottenham.

Moments later the teams made their way out onto the pitch. There was a cheer, albeit a bit of a half-hearted one, from the home fans, and a more enthusiastic one from the hundred or so away fans who'd made the long journey from Stimport, as the two sides walked out side-by-side behind the referee and linesmen.

'What are Stimport Rangers like?' asked Nelson.

'Mid-table,' answered Danny, who, as he always did, had been studying Chadmouth's opponents all week to assess his team's chances. 'They've drawn their last four. Tough to beat, but they don't score many goals.'

The players and officials shook hands and the ref tossed a coin. Chadmouth would kick off.

The ref blew his whistle and Ferguson kicked the ball back to Parker to get the match underway.

Chapter 9

Less than a minute later Chadmouth were behind. Stimport's winger left Duffy, Chadmouth's right back, for dead, and crossed to his completely unmarked team-mate who calmly headed into the net. Groans and boos rang out around the ground. It was the worst possible start, and it was soon to become even worse.

With ten minutes on the clock, Stimport put together a neat passing move that the Chadmouth defence had no answer to. A shot from the edge of the box was saved by Mortensen, but the ball fell straight to a Stimport player who easily tapped it in to make it 2-0. The boos were even louder this time, and many angry fans were shouting abuse at the players they felt were letting them down. The away fans, needless to say, were loving it.

'Our luck's going to turn today is it Dad?' said Danny sarcastically. 'Three points today, do you reckon?'

'Yeah, well *you* said Stimport didn't score many goals,' Dad snapped back.

Danny felt sorry for Nelson. What had they brought him along to? He didn't seem too bothered though. It wasn't his team that was heading for the drop, was it? He was checking his phone from time to time, looking up the scores from the Premiership.

'Liverpool are still nil-nil with Spurs,' he told Danny.

'Great,' said Danny, sounding like it was anything but great. Nelson got the hint and didn't give him any more updates after that.

The rest of the first half was pretty rubbish, and nothing much else happened, and everyone was glad when the half-time whistle blew. The teams left the pitch for the safety of the dressing room, accompanied by another round of boos. Nippy the Crab, very wisely in Danny's opinion, gave his usual half-time walk around the ground a miss.

Dad sighed.

'Do you want to stay or go?' he asked the boys.

'Go?! We can't go,' said Danny, shocked. 'We never leave before the end.'

'I was just thinking of Nelson,' explained Dad. 'This can't be much fun for him.'

'I'm alright,' said Nelson. 'Don't worry about me.'

'We're staying,' said Danny firmly.

'Okay,' said Dad. 'I wouldn't want to have to tell Gran we didn't stick it out anyway.'

'So much for our luck dance,' Nelson whispered to Danny.

'What was that?' asked Dad.

'Nothing,' said Danny, giving Nelson a warning look. He didn't want his dad laughing at them, not in the mood he was in after that first half.

The teams were soon back out for the second half. There was a strange atmosphere as they got back underway. It was as if the Chadmouth fans had all accepted that the game was up, and they were going down. As if nothing really mattered anymore. Danny had never seen anything like it, but he wasn't surprised. You could only believe in a lost cause for so long. Nelson even felt it was safe to tell Danny that Liverpool had just gone a goal up in their match. It was quiet, with not even much booing of mistakes or abusing the referee going on, and the players on both teams seemed to be going through the motions too.

That was, however, until about twenty minutes into the second half. Chadmouth were given a free kick about five metres outside the penalty area, for a foul on their captain, Sanchez. It was within range for Logan, their dead-ball specialist, if you could call someone who'd scored one goal all season from a free-kick a dead-ball specialist. Still, he placed the ball carefully on the ground as if he regularly curled them into the top corner of the net, as the ref paced out the distance for the Stimport wall to stand behind. The possibility of a rare strike on goal had got most of the crowd's attention, apart from the man with no shirt, who was more interested in trying to wind up the opposition fans with a rude chant.

'Straight into the wall,' predicted one of the men behind them.

'Straight over the top of the stand more like,' disagreed his friend.

The ref blew his whistle. Logan took a few steps back and started his run-up. He ran up to the ball and smacked it as hard as he could. It was a dreadful strike and looked more likely to hit the corner flag than the back of the net, but then something amazing happened. The ball hit one of the Stimport defenders, bounced off the side of his head and flew towards the goal. It smacked into the post, ricocheted onto the goalie, and into the net.

There was as much laughter as there were cheers. It was one of the worst goals ever seen at Springly Park, but they all counted, and it was now 2-1.

Danny looked at Nelson, and Nelson looked at Danny. You couldn't say that that goal had been anything other than lucky. Chadmouth were still losing though, and it would be nothing but a consolation goal if they couldn't find one, and preferably two more. It seemed unlikely, but the team did look to have a bit more belief now, and the crowd was starting to get behind them again.

Chadmouth began to dominate possession and put pressure on the Stimport goal during the next twenty minutes. Wilson went close with a long-range effort, and Speirs missed a header from a corner that he really should have put away.

'How...' Danny started to ask.

'Five minutes,' Dad told him, anticipating his question. 'You didn't forget your...'

'Oh no, it's alright, I've got it,' said Danny, remembering that he had his phone this week and checking how long was left himself.

Chadmouth continued to press, and Ferguson was denied by a last-ditch challenge when it looked like he was going to be through on goal.

Time was running out, and a few supporters began to leave, thinking their team was about to record yet another defeat. Normal time was just about up when Duffy thumped a hopeful ball down the right-wing. Right-winger Wilson managed to get there first and cut inside the defender. He looked for someone to pass to, but the only player up with him was Osborne, who was hopelessly offside. Wilson fired in a cross anyway, and the Stimport defence all appealed for offside. The whistle didn't go though, and Osborne had the ball on the edge of the six-yard box. The crowd held its breath and rose to its feet. He couldn't miss from there, could he? He drew his foot back, shot, and the back of the net bulged.

The crowd went wild, and Danny and Dad leapt up and down as if they'd just won the World Cup. Nelson joined in the celebrations too. The Stimport players were furiously telling the ref that Osborne was miles offside, which, to be fair, he had been. The ref was waving them away though, and eventually showed the red card to the Stimport goalie for protesting too much. Osborne grabbed the ball out of the net and raced back to the halfway line, ready for the restart. It was already the come-back of the season. They couldn't score a winner as well could they?

Chapter 10

Normal time was up. They were into stoppage time now, and the fourth official had just indicated there would be just three minutes. Three minutes. Three minutes to find an unlikely winner that might, just might, save Chadmouth's season.

Stimport were down to ten men having had their goalie sent off, and one of their outfield players had had to go in goal as they'd already used all their subs, but was there enough time for Chadmouth to take advantage? Only two minutes to go now. Everyone had stayed on their feet. Chadmouth hit the ball into the Stimport box, but their stand-in keeper managed to grab hold of it. Danny realised that he'd been holding his breath.

One minute left. It should have been remembered as a famous comeback, even if it ended 2-2, but a point just wasn't enough. They really needed all three points. Thirty seconds to go. It only takes a second to score a goal, the commentators often said, but that was almost all that was left.

Suddenly, out of nowhere, Chadmouth won a corner. Everyone piled into the Stimport box, even Mortensen, who came up from the Chadmouth goal. Stimport had everyone back too. The corner came in. It wasn't bad, but it looked like the stand-in keeper was going to catch it. He jumped high, got his hands to the ball... and dropped it. Players from both sides flew in as the ball landed on the goal-line, desperate to hack it clear or poke it in. The ball flew around, off one boot, then another. There were so many bodies around it that it was hard to see what was happening, but then...

'YESSSSSSSSSSSSSSSSSS!!!'

Unbelievably, the ball was in the net. The referee confirmed that it was a goal, and the crowd now really did go wild. Men, women, boys and girls were jumping up and down, shouting, screaming, punching the air and hugging anybody and everybody within reach. Danny found himself hugging Nelson, which normally would have embarrassed them both, but at that point, he really didn't care.

The visitors trudged back to the halfway line, kicked off, and the ref blew up for full-time, starting the cheering again just as it had been starting to die down.

The ground slowly started to empty, with everyone who was there to support the home team leaving with a big smile on their face.

'Told you our luck would turn today,' said Dad to Danny as they made their way down the steps at the back of the stand. 'About time too,' he added before turning to chat to a couple of fellow supporters he knew.

'He's right,' Danny said to Nelson with a knowing grin. 'We were definitely lucky today. That's got to be one of the greatest comebacks ever.'

'It was pretty amazing,' Nelson agreed. 'I think my dad would still tell you Liverpool's Champions League final comeback was better though.'

'Oh yeah, he definitely would.'

'"Have I ever told you about the time I was there to see the Miracle of Istanbul?"' said Nelson, doing a very good impression of his dad. Danny laughed.

'So did Liverpool win in the end?' Danny asked Nelson.

'In Istanbul?'

'No, today.'

'Oh, I forgot to check the final score,' said Nelson, pulling his phone out of his pocket. 'Finished one-nil,' he said after a few seconds.

'One-nil? So boring,' Danny told him with a smile. 'You'll have to keep coming here if you want a bit more excitement.'

'It only happened because I *was* here,' Nelson told him. 'Or at least because of what we did before the match,' he added with a wink.

'What was that?' asked Dad, breaking away from his conversation briefly.

'Oh, nothing,' answered Danny. 'You're right though,' he said to Nelson when he was sure his dad was no longer listening to them, 'we made that happen I reckon.'

'You actually believe that?'

'Yeah. Why, don't you?'

'We can't have done really, can we?'

'We must have done. We've never been that lucky before.'

'I dunno. Maybe.'

Danny wondered, had they really just influenced the result, or was it just a coincidence? Did their strange dance have some kind of magical power?

'We're off the bottom of the table now aren't we?' asked Dad, who'd ended his conversation now as his friends had got back to their car.

Danny looked up the updated league table on his phone.

'Yeah,' he told the others with a broad smile. 'One point above Marshfield now. Only six points from safety. We could do this you know.'

Calthorpe Borough 2-0 Beddingley City
Chadmouth Town 3-2 Stimport Rangers
Finbury Rovers 2-3 Throckmorton Town
Kenton Athletic 1-3 Blueport City
Burbank Rovers 1-1 Marshfield County
Plumborough Town 0-0 Redrick Wanderers

		Played	Won	Drawn	Lost	GD	Points
19	Finbury	39	10	7	22	-20	37
20	Beddingley	39	8	11	20	-15	35
21	Plumborough	39	6	14	19	-28	32
22	Kenton	39	6	11	22	-30	29
23	Chadmouth	39	6	11	22	-29	29
24	Marshfield	39	5	13	21	-34	28

Chapter 11

Later that evening, Danny made a decision. He was convinced that what they'd done before the match really had given Chadmouth the luck they'd been sorely missing. It must be some sort of magic, or maybe he had some sort of superpower he never knew about. That was the only explanation, and he was determined to do it again before the next match. If he didn't, they'd probably go back to being unlucky and losing. It was down to him, but he was going to need the stuff they'd used earlier. He surprised his parents by telling them he was off for a run, changed into shorts and trainers, grabbed an empty Sainsbury's bag from the kitchen cupboard, and jogged back to the park. He was desperately hoping everything would still be there, and was relieved to find that it was.

He felt a bit stupid picking it up and putting it in his bag, but it was something he had to do. There was nobody else there to see him anyway. In went the old trainer, then the broken umbrella. He carefully picked up the black dog-poo bag using the stick, checked that it was extremely well knotted, and dropped it into the Sainsbury's bag. He popped the stick in as well and headed for home.

When he got back he stashed the bag behind some old plant pots in the shed, locked the door, and went back indoors. He was ready for the next home match.

* * *

Danny hated hospitals. Of course, nobody particularly liked them, but he *really* disliked them. He was there to visit Gran, who'd taken a turn for the worse over the weekend. Everyone was being a bit vague about what was wrong with her. All he'd been told was that she wasn't feeling very well but it wasn't anything serious and she'd probably be allowed back home after a few days of rest. He was happy to believe that.

Danny and Dad stepped out of the lift and studied the signs on the wall opposite them, trying to work out how to get to Gran's ward.

'This way, I think,' said Dad, and set off along the corridor. Danny followed him, holding the bunch of flowers and the bag of grapes that they'd brought with them, which Dad had said was you had to bring whenever you visited anyone in hospital.

They soon came to the ward they'd been told Gran was on, and they went in and looked around for her. They soon spotted her in the bed nearest the window.

'Hi Gran,' called Danny as he made his way over to her bed, waking up at least three other elderly ladies who had been sleeping in the other beds on the ward. They didn't look too pleased, but Gran certainly did. Her face lit up to see her son and grandson, and she started to sit up in bed. That made her start coughing though.

'Here, let me help,' said Dad, adjusting her pillows as Danny sat down on the chair next to her.

'We got you these,' he told her, placing the flowers and grapes on the side of the bed.

'Oh, thank you, sweetie,' she answered with a smile.

Dad went to borrow a chair from next to another bed whose occupant was fast asleep and snoring loudly, and an eagle-eyed nurse who had obviously spotted their arrival brought over a vase and put the flowers in for Gran, placing it on the cabinet next to her bed.

'So, how are you feeling now Mum?' Dad asked her.

'Never mind how I'm feeling,' she told him, sounding a bit croaky. 'How are *you* both feeling after the comeback of the century on Saturday?'

That was typical Gran, more interested in her beloved Chadmouth Town than her own health.

'It was amazing Gran,' Danny told her. 'Absolutely incredible. We were behind in the first minute, dreadful defending, as usual, then 2-0 down after ten, then, mid-way through the second half, Logan hit a terrible free-kick that was going well wide but it hit their defender on the head and went in, but we couldn't score a second until the final minute of normal time, when Osborne scored, even though he was probably offside. Oh, and they had their goalie sent off. Then, deep in injury time now, we won a corner, and the ball bounced around in their box forever, until somehow Ferguson put it in the net. 3-2 to us. The greatest comeback ever!'

Chapter 12

Gran smiled as she followed every word of Danny's summary. She could see the joy the win had given him.

'It's just a shame you weren't able to be there,' said Dad.

'Oh, I was there in spirit,' she told him. 'And I was listening to the commentary on the radio. I thought the commentator was going to explode when the winner went in.'

'I think *we* nearly did,' said Dad.

'Are you going to be well enough to go to the Eastbury Albion match?' Danny asked her.

'Well now, we'll have to see won't we,' said Gran. 'I've got to get out of this place first.'

'We could smuggle you out,' Danny said. 'I saw this film once where this man wanted to get this other man out of hospital, even though he was under police guard because he was a gangster or a serial killer or something, I can't remember, so he stole a white coat and a stethoscope and disguised himself as a doctor, found a wheelchair, bandaged the gangster (or serial killer) guy's face up, and just wheeled him out of there.'

'Well,' Gran chuckled, 'it's one option. I'll get back to you on that if that's okay?'

'Yeah, fine,' said Danny, wondering whether Nelson would give him a hand stealing his gran.

'Any idea when you'll be ready to go home?' Dad asked.

'They don't tell me anything,' Gran moaned.

'Do you want me to find a doctor to ask?'

'Oh yes please love.'

Dad wandered off to find a doctor. Danny helped himself to some grapes.

'So, do you think our luck's turned then?' Gran asked him.

Danny thought about telling her how he and Nelson's luck dance had made them have good luck, but thought better of it. She'd probably only laugh.

'I hope so. It's about time it did.'

'The commentators always say that luck evens itself out over the season,' said Gran.

'Dad said that too.'

'I've never believed that myself.'

'We were definitely lucky on Saturday though,' said Danny. 'All three of our goals were just like the ones teams have been scoring *against* us all season.'

'Well, maybe it is starting to even itself out, like they say. I just hope it's not too late.'

'We're not down yet.'

'No Danny, we're not down yet,' said Gran with a twinkle in her eye.

Just then Dad came back with a doctor in tow. The doctor stopped at the end of the bed and took a look at the notes on the clipboard that was hooked over the end. She studied them for a moment before putting them back and going round to the side of the bed.

'Good news Mrs Mann,' she told her patient. 'It looks like the antibiotics are doing the trick and the infection's clearing up nicely. A couple more days in here, just so we can keep an eye on you, and you'll be ready to go home I reckon.'

'Will she be able to go to the match?' asked Danny hopefully. 'It's a week on Saturday?'

The doctor smiled.

'Football? I wouldn't advise it. This has taken a lot out of your gran. I think she needs to take it a bit easy for a few weeks.'

'A few weeks?' said Gran, looking aghast. 'I can't stay away for that long. My team needs me.'

'I really would advise it, Mrs Mann,' insisted the doctor. 'You need to look after yourself at your age.'

'At my age? I don't know what you mean,' said Gran. 'I'll have you know I'm the fittest by a country mile at my keep-fit class.'

'Don't worry doctor,' said Dad, seeing the look of concern on her face. 'I'll make sure she doesn't do anything silly.'

'Hmmph! We'll see about that,' said Gran with a frown.

Chapter 13

'You're joking. You can come really, can't you?' Danny asked Nelson, as they sat next to each other in the hall eating lunch. Danny had just been filling Nelson in on Chadmouth's latest disappointing result, a 1-0 defeat away to Redrick Wanderers that left them second-bottom, still six points from safety, before checking that Nelson could go to their next home game.

'No, I really can't,' said Nelson. 'It's my sister's wedding in a few weeks time. I've got to go for a fitting?'

'For your bridesmaid's dress?'

'Very funny. No. They're making me wear a suit.'

'Can't you do that another time?'

'Apparently not. Come on, you know how important weddings are in my family. We've only just recovered from my brother's last year.'

'Yeah, okay,' sighed Danny. 'But I can't believe you're going to miss the Eastbury game on Saturday.'

'You're assuming I wanted to go anyway,' Nelson pointed out.

'Course you wanted to go. After what happened against Stimport? You're going to every home game from now on.'

'Apart from this one. Is your gran still ill then?'

'Yeah. She's back home now, but she's not well enough to go to football yet.'

'Right. Well, you're going to have a spare ticket then I'm afraid, unless you can persuade someone else to come with you. You could ask Ashton.'

'Yeah, right,' said Danny, glancing round at Ashton and his annoying mates, who were thankfully too busy trying to knock over the smaller kids with their football to be giving Danny any abuse. 'Anyway, it's not just about going to the match. We've got to do the luck dance beforehand.'

'You're not still going on about that are you?' said Nelson.

'Of course I'm still going on about it. It worked, didn't it?'

'No Danny, it didn't work. You just got lucky.'

'Exactly! We got lucky *because* we did the luck dance.'

'Do you really believe that us stomping around like idiots in the park made the Crabs win?'

'Yes! Think about it. We've had the worst luck in the world, ever, all season. Then we do the luck dance, we suddenly get the most incredible luck and we win the match. What else could it have been?'

'Just… luck?'

'You said you believed it on Saturday.'

'Yeah, but… At the time it seemed like it could have been us, but…'

'But nothing. It was us. It was our luck dance. I know it.'

'I dunno.'

'I don't know how, but I reckon we've stumbled across some sort of football magic. It was your idea to do it, anyway. You can't turn your back on it now.'

'Maybe. But anyway, I can't go on Saturday. So you'll have to do it without me.'

'But it might not work if it's just me.'

'Well, there's only one way to find out.'

'That's no good. This isn't the time for experiments. This is life or death for Chadmouth Town.'

'Well, not quite life or death.'

'As good as. If we lose because you didn't do the luck dance…'

'Stop blaming me...'

'We could be 9 points from safety with only 3 games left. It'll take a miracle to escape from there.'

'Okay. I'll have another word with my mum, but I know what she'll say.'

'Thanks. I'm relying on you Nelson. All of Chadmouth Town is relying on you.'

'Oh, great. So no pressure then.'

Redrick Wanderers 1-0 Chadmouth Town
Beddingley City 1-4 Timton United
Estonpark Borough 2-2 Kenton Athletic
Finbury Rovers 0-1 Fishton Grove
Marshfield County 0-2 Allerborough United
Sturton Town 1-1 Plumborough Town

	Played	Won	Drawn	Lost	GD	Points
19 Finbury	40	10	7	23	-21	37
20 Beddingley	40	8	11	21	-18	35
21 Plumborough	40	6	15	19	-28	33
22 Kenton	40	6	12	22	-30	30
23 Chadmouth	40	6	11	23	-35	29
24 Marshfield	40	5	13	22	-33	28

Chapter 14

It was no good though. Nelson's mum was having none of it, and he messaged Danny on Friday evening to say he definitely wasn't allowed to go. Danny was just going to have to do it on his own.

He got up late on Saturday morning, ate some chocolate spread on toast for breakfast, had a shower and put on his Chadmouth shirt. With nothing much else to do before the match he told his parents he was just going for a ride on his bike, and set off to do the luck dance in the park. He got his bike out of the shed, along with the Sainsbury's bag containing the stick, trainer, brolly and dog-poo bag. Hooking the bag over his handlebars he quickly cycled to the park.

He was pleased to see that there was no one else there again, as he lay his bike down on the grass where they'd done the luck dance before. He carefully emptied out the bag and wondered which of the things to hold. Should he just hold the brolly and trainer as he had before, or should he try to hold Nelson's dog-poo bag on a stick too? Eventually, he decided to go with the trainer and the dog-poo bag on a stick, and he then realised he wasn't sure he could remember all of Nelson's chant.

He tried running through it in his head.

'Fi. Fi fie. Fi fie fo. Kumala. Vista. Kumala kumala kumala vista. Oh la-noh la-noh la-vista. Eenie meenie dessameenie ooh-aah ooh-orrameenie. Beep deedly....'

Oh no. He couldn't remember the last line. It definitely wouldn't work if he couldn't even finish the chant. He quickly grabbed his phone and messaged Nelson, hoping he had his phone on.

WHAT COMES AFTER BEEP DEEDLY?

His phone pinged an agonising minute later.

ODEN BODEN BODASH SKADUTENDATEN

That was it. He messaged back thanks to Nelson.

Right. It was time to do it, now he knew what to do. He picked up the trainer and the stick, hooked the dog-poo bag on the end, and started striding round in a circle, waving them above his head. He started the chant.

'Fi. Fi fie. Fi fie fo.'

Something didn't seem right though, and not just because Nelson wasn't there. Then he remembered – t-shirt over the head. He stopped, pulled his shirt up, then carried on.

'Fi. Fi fie. Fi fie fo. Kumala. Vista. Kumala kumala kumala vista. Oh la-noh la-noh la-vista. Eenie meenie dessameenie ooh-aah ooh-orrameenie. Beep deedly oden boden bodash skadutendaten.'

He did it a couple of times, including the bit where he got down on his knees and asked the gods of football for their help, then stopped. It wasn't anywhere near as funny this time, and he wondered whether that was because he was on his own or because he now knew how important it was to Chadmouth's season. There was no thunder or rainbow either, but maybe that only happened the first time you did it. Hopefully it had worked though. He put his stuff back in the bag, put the bag back on the handlebars, and cycled home to have some lunch before setting off with Dad.

* * *

A couple of hours later Danny and his dad were on their way to the match. Dad chose the route this time and took them down Church Street. They bought a programme, today from a man with glasses as thick as binoculars who just grunted when they gave him the money, and Dad waited while Danny popped to the toilet before taking their usual seats, waiting for the Crabs to take on Eastbury Albion.

'It doesn't seem right, does it?' said Dad, pointing to Gran's empty seat.

'No,' Danny agreed.

Dad studied the programme for a bit while Danny listened to the two men who sat behind them.

'We're bound to get thrashed today,' said the first. 'Always happens in our next home game after a comeback win.'

'No it doesn't,' argued the other. 'We came from 2-0 down after ten minutes against Plumborough a few years back, then won our next one against Burbank.'

'No we didn't. They spanked us 4-0.'

'They never did. We've never lost 4-0 to Burbank Rovers. You're thinking of Finbury Rovers.'

'I am not. We've never lost to them by more than one goal.'

Danny wondered which one of them, if either, was right. It was like they'd been watching different teams. They stopped arguing as the two teams came out onto the pitch.

Chapter 15

A louder cheer than Danny had heard for a while greeted them. The fans must have started to believe again after their dramatic victory last weekend had taken them off the bottom of the table, even though they'd lost their next away game. Dad noticed it too.

'Looks like everyone's got a bit of hope back,' he said to Danny when the noise had died down a bit. 'It's a dangerous thing though, hope.'

'Why's that?' asked Danny.

'It means it hurts even more when you lose,' Dad explained.

Danny thought that was a bit negative, but he kind of knew what Dad meant. He was more nervous than usual today. What if the luck dance didn't work without Nelson? What if he'd done it wrong? If Chadmouth lost today it would be all his fault.

Ten minutes after kick-off he wasn't so worried about them losing. Their opponents were rubbish. They were struggling to string more than two passes together and the closest they'd come to scoring was a corner that had been so badly overhit it had gone out for a throw-in on the opposite side of the pitch.

The only problem was, Chadmouth weren't a lot better. They were having most of the possession but were panicking whenever they got anywhere near the Eastbury penalty area, either firing long-range efforts into row Z of the stand or trying overly ambitious passes that just gave the ball away to their opponents.

After another ten minutes, the crowd started to become restless. They thought their team should be ahead by now, and knew only too well that one mistake at the back, like they'd been making all season, would see them fall behind, and that could be enough to lose the match.

No one seemed unhappy to hear the half-time whistle, and the crowd happily trooped off to buy their half-time drinks and snacks, hoping that Wedlock, their manager, could get his team playing in the second half a bit more like the team that had finished the last home match so strongly.

The second half carried on pretty much the same as the first though. On the hour mark, Wedlock decided he needed to change things, and made a double substitution, bringing on Mutch and Roscamp for Wilson and Parker. It made no difference though. Chadmouth did have a shot on target, but Burbanks' strike was straight at the Eastbury goalie. Eastbury had an effort of their own that flew narrowly wide, which got the Crabs fans biting their nails, then Chadmouth had a claim for a penalty when Ferguson went down in the box, but nobody really seemed to think it was a foul. Danny wondered whether the ref would have given it anyway if he and Nelson had done the luck dance together though.

With ten minutes to go Chadmouth made their last change, with Houchen replacing Sagar. It was a brave move by Wedlock, bringing on a striker for a defender, but they really had nothing to lose now. They needed to win, and if they lost that wasn't a lot worse than a draw at this stage in the season.

'Should have done that twenty minutes ago,' grumbled Dad.

Time was running out. Could Chadmouth score another dramatic late winner? The crowd were urging them forward every time they had the ball, but their hopeful long balls were all being dealt with comfortably by the Eastbury defence, who seemed happy to settle for a draw. The frustrated Crabs supporters were singing 'Boring boring Eastbury!' but it wasn't bothering their opponents in the slightest, and a few minutes later they'd earned their draw, with the match finishing 0-0.

The crowd wasn't sure how to greet the result. It was a point, which might be valuable, but they really needed three. Their team hadn't been able to follow up on their previous result, and their chances of survival still looked bleak.

'Well, that was dull,' said Dad as they made their way out of the stadium.

'I've seen better,' agreed Danny.

He was still wondering if it might have been different if Nelson had been with him and they'd done the luck dance properly. Would that penalty have been given? He wasn't 100% sure he believed in the power of the luck dance, but there was one thing he was sure of – he was going to do everything he possibly could to keep the Crabs up.

Chadmouth Town 0-0 Eastbury Albion
Blueport City 2-0 Finbury Rovers
Fishton Grove 2-1 Beddingley City
Kenton Athletic 3-3 Northford
Plumborough Town 2-0 Swaffbury Rangers
Parkbridge United 1-1 Marshfield County

		Played	Won	Drawn	Lost	GD	Points
19	Finbury	41	10	7	24	-23	37
20	Plumborough	41	7	15	19	-26	36
21	Beddingley	41	8	11	22	-19	35
22	Kenton	41	6	13	22	-30	31
23	Chadmouth	41	6	12	23	-35	30
24	Marshfield	41	5	14	22	-33	29

Chapter 16

Danny couldn't concentrate. He was supposed to be writing a book review on *The Twits*, but he couldn't stop thinking about what had happened in the last two matches he'd seen. The first one they'd won, but only because they'd been incredibly lucky, which was something that hadn't happened all season. But there was no luck on show in the second one, although, to be fair, they hadn't had any bad luck either.

He couldn't work out whether he and Nelson had had anything to do with it. They'd done their luck dance for the first match, and they'd been lucky, and he'd tried to do it on his own for the second, when they hadn't been lucky or unlucky. Maybe it had worked a bit, but not enough. Maybe it had to be done exactly the same each time or it wouldn't work.

Did that mean *exactly* the same though? He was sure it needed both of them to do the luck dance, in the same place, with the same stick, poo-bag, trainer and brolly, but what else needed to be the same? He started to think about what else they'd done that day. There was quite a lot when he thought about it, so he started to make a list.

- Me and Nelson
- Luck dance - trainer, umbrella, stick and poo bag, shirts over heads
- Walk down Hope Street to Kingsley Park
- Buy programme from lady with bobble hat and say the same things
- Nelson to go the toilet but not me
- Same breakfast (weetabix me + whatever Nelson had before)
- Same clothes (both of us)
- Cheese rolls and pickled onion monster munch for lunch

Now that he thought about it, even though he'd tried to do the luck dance on his own, he realised that quite a bit had been different, as well as Nelson not being there. He hadn't been wearing the same jeans, and he'd had toast for breakfast and a different lunch too. It was all wrong. They'd walked down Church Street rather than Hope Street, bought a programme from a different seller, and Danny had even gone to the toilet before kick-off. That must be why they hadn't won.

Of course, he couldn't be sure that it was *all* important, but there was no way of knowing what was and what wasn't. They'd just have to do every single thing the same, just in case. He'd speak to Nelson as soon as he could and tell him his plan - his plan to save Chadmouth Town from relegation.

Chapter 17

Danny sat on the opposite side of the class to Nelson, so he had to wait until morning break to speak to his friend. He hadn't wanted to join in the football match that, as usual, was being played. He'd had enough of the taunts of the Prem Gang. He sat on the bench in the corner of the playground with Nelson, filling him in on the highlights of Saturday's game, which hadn't taken him long.

'Doesn't sound like I missed much then,' said Nelson.

'Not really.'

'Still sounds more interesting than the wedding fitting though.'

'Oh yeah, how did it go?'

'Alright. A lot of hanging around and people getting stupidly excited about clothes. I'd rather have watched a whole day's worth of goalless football than that.'

'We could have played for a whole day and not scored I reckon,' said Danny. 'We didn't have any amazing luck like we did against Stimport.'

'You wait all season for a bit of luck, then it's gone, never to happen again,' moaned Nelson.

'Yeah,' said Danny, 'but I think we can change that.'

'What? Oh no, you're not on about that stupid luck dance again, are you? Didn't you do it on Saturday?'

'Yeah, but not properly.'

'What do you mean?'

'It was just me, not both of us.'

'You actually think it worked when we both did it?'

'It must have done. The only time we did it together we were lucky. Every other match, when we've not done it, we've been unlucky. I did it on my own and it only worked enough to stop us being unlucky. That proves it doesn't it?'

'Um...'

'It does Nelson. It means we have to do it, together, properly, before each match until the end of the season. It's the only way we're going to stay up. I know it.'

'Well, what about away matches? You're not planning to go to them are you?'

'I don't know. I might speak to Dad about it.'

'Well, I definitely won't be allowed to go to away games. They might let me go to some more home matches, but not away ones.'

'You'll come to the rest of the home games then?'

'I never said that.'

'You kind of did. Come on Nelson. I need you. Chadmouth needs you.'

'Well, okay, I guess.'

'Brilliant. And we have to do the luck dance again, exactly the same. Actually, I've worked it out. We have to do everything the same.'

'What do you mean, everything?'

'Absolutely everything. Everything we both did before the Stimport match.

'What are you talking about?'

Danny got the list he'd made earlier out of his pocket.

'Right, we've both got to eat the same breakfast when we get up, wear the same clothes…'

'What, even the same pants?'

'Good point, I hadn't thought of that. Yes, even the same pants.'

'Argh, why didn't I keep my big mouth shut?'

'Then you need to come over to mine in the morning so we can go to the park and do the luck dance, exactly the same as we did before with the same brolly, trainer, stick and poo-bag…'

'You went back and got them didn't you?'

'Yeah.'

'Even that bagful of poo?'

'Well, yeah. It's tied up tight.'

'Mate!'

'Then we need to go back home, eat the same lunch, take the same route to Springly Park, buy a programme from the same programme seller and have the same conversation with her, you go to the toilet but not me, then we watch the match.'

'Are you sure that's everything? Do I have to breathe the same number of times, or fart and burp at the right time?'

'Don't be stupid.'

'Sorry, silly me.'

'So you'll do it then?'

'Oh, if I have to.'

'Yes! Thanks, Nelson. This is going to work, I know it.'

'Well, I hope you're right. It had better be worth it. When's the next match?'

'A week Saturday. We're away to Libley United this week.'

'Right. I'll check I can go when I get home. I don't think we've got any more fittings or anything now.'

'Cool. I've worked out how many points we'll have if we can win our last three home games, even if we lose all the away ones, and what I think the teams above us will get, and I reckon three wins will be enough to keep us up.'

'If only you could think of a way to influence everyone else's results as well,' said Nelson, before immediately regretting it. 'Before you ask – no. If you think of something you want to try, you're on your own.'

Chapter 18

'Dad,' said Danny as he sat down for tea that evening with his parents, 'can we go to the game at Libley on Saturday?'

'What?' snorted Dad. 'That nil-nil draw was so good it's left you wanting to go to away games as well has it?'

'It's not that. It's just, every match is so important now. I'd just like to be there. That's all.'

'Well, I don't fancy a three hundred mile round trip to watch us play rubbish and lose, thank you very much.'

'We might not play rubbish and lose.'

'No, but we're not likely to win either are we, let's face it. We've only won once away all season.'

'But Dad…'

'No Danny,' said Dad firmly. 'The answer's no. You'll just have to listen on the radio like you usually do.'

Danny wasn't too upset. He'd been expecting that to be Dad's answer. There was no harm in asking though.

They ate in silence for a while.

'How was school Danny?' asked his mum after a while.

'Okay.'

'Still getting trouble from those boys?' she asked him.

'Not really,' he lied. He didn't bother mentioning that one of the Prem Gang was a girl either.

'Well, let me know if you want me to have a word with the school.'

'Okay,' he lied again. That was the last thing he wanted, especially as his parents would probably be told about him getting into trouble last week for attacking Ashton. The Prem Gang were annoying, but he could handle it.

They finished eating and Dad cleared the plates away to load up the dishwasher. Danny helped himself to an ice cream from the freezer and sat back down to eat it. He'd almost finished it by the time Dad sat back down.

'Dad, have you got anything that you always do before a game, you know, for luck?'

'Um, no. Why?'

'Oh, they were talking about that sort of thing on that football podcast I listen to the other day.'

'Oh, right. Well, lots of fans do have superstitions. I read about a guy once who always turned the commentary off when he watched a match on TV and had a "songs from Disney films" playlist playing in the background for the entire match instead, just because his team had won once whilst his kids were listening to it. Weird.'

'Yeah, weird.'

'Lots of players are massively superstitious too. Liverpool players all touch the Welcome to Anfield sign in the tunnel on their way out to matches for example.'

'Oh yeah, I think Nelson's mentioned that,' said Danny, making a note to mention that if Nelson had second thoughts and needed persuading.

'Cristiano Ronaldo always has to be the last one onto the pitch, and he steps onto the grass right foot first then jumps up in the air. Watch him next time he's on telly. Johan Cruyff, (you've heard of him right?), he always used to spit his chewing gum into the opposition half before the match. Disgusting really. When France won the World Cup in 1998 their captain kissed the top of their goalie's bald head before every match. Superstitious idiots. Hah - superstidiots!' he laughed. Danny didn't.

Danny had been wondering whether to mention his new pre-match ritual to his dad, to see what he thought about it. He decided it was probably best if he didn't.

Chapter 19

Danny's dad hadn't changed his mind about going to Libley to watch the match on Saturday, so instead the two of them were glued to the radio in their front room, listening to their local radio station's commentary.

'I hate listening to matches,' said Danny.

'You're not still going on about wanting to go to the game are you?' grumbled Dad.

'No. I just don't like not being able to see what's happening.'

'Yeah, I know what you mean. It's better than nothing though isn't it?'

'I suppose.'

The commentator described the kick-off and the opening stages of the match. It was a game Chadmouth really couldn't afford to lose.

The first half was just about bearable for Danny, with not too much goal-mouth incident at either end of the pitch, but things took a turn for the worse early in the second half when the Crabs failed to clear a corner and Libley scored. They weren't behind for long though, with Sanchez slipping the ball to Ferguson on the edge of the box and his shot past the Libley keeper equalising for Chadmouth.

All the excitement was packed into those few short minutes though. Neither team came close to scoring a winner and the final score was 1-1.

'That could have been worse,' said Dad.

'Could have been better too,' pointed out Danny.

He checked the scores from the matches involving the other teams at the bottom of League One. All of the teams just above Chadmouth had drawn except Plumborough, who had lost, so Chadmouth now needed to make up five points to avoid relegation. They only had four matches left now in which to do it though.

'Every match is a cup-final now,' said Dad. Danny knew exactly what he meant.

Beddingley City 0-0 Fieldbridge Wanderers
Finbury Rovers 2-2 Allerborough United
Libley United 1-1 Chadmouth Town
Marshfield County 1-4 Greaseworth City
Potterton United 0-0 Kenton Athletic
Timton United 1-0 Plumborough Town

		Played	Won	Drawn	Lost	GD	Points
19	Finbury	42	10	8	24	-23	38
20	Beddingley	42	8	12	22	-19	36
21	Plumborough	42	7	15	20	-27	36
22	Kenton	42	6	14	22	-30	32
23	Chadmouth	42	6	13	23	-35	31
24	Marshfield	42	5	14	23	-36	29

Chapter 20

'Oh wow, you really did keep them then,' said Nelson, as Danny got the Sainsbury's bag out of the shed and showed him the stick with the V shape in the end, old trainer, broken umbrella and dog-poo bag, still tied up tightly.

'Do you have any idea how valuable these are?' Danny asked him.

'Bit weird though.'

'Maybe. Who cares though, as long as it works.'

'I guess.'

'Come on, we need to get to the park.'

'Okay. Let's get it over with.'

'Believe me, Nelson. It works. It really works.'

'How can it though?'

'I don't know. I just know that it does. It's magic, you're not meant to understand how it works.'

'I was just messing when I made it up though.'

'I know, but you've obviously discovered something amazing, somehow.'

Nelson grunted, unconvinced, as they set off towards the park, with Danny carrying his plastic bag as if it contained the Crown Jewels. He'd been happy to join in the first time, it had been a laugh, but Danny was taking it all a bit too seriously now in his opinion. He'd already had to start the day with beans on toast for breakfast, as he'd told Danny that's what he'd had on the morning of the Stimport Rangers match, and Danny had told him to wear the same t-shirt, jeans and trainers. He'd had no problem with the jeans and trainers, but Danny had sent him home to change his t-shirt because the one he'd worn before was dirty and he'd put on a different one. Fortunately, he only lived around the corner, and his mum hadn't seen him leaving the house wearing the t-shirt with ketchup stains down the front that he'd rescued from the wash-basket.

'You have got the same pants and socks on as well, haven't you?' asked Danny.

'Yes! I told you. Do you want to check them?'

'No, you're alright. I don't know what ones you had on last time anyway.'

'They're the same, okay, trust me.'

'Okay.'

Soon they were at the park, and Danny led them straight to the luck-dance spot. Danny emptied out the bag and handed Nelson his stick.

'I can't believe we're actually doing this again,' moaned Nelson, shaking his head.

'Come on,' said Danny, ignoring him. 'Scoop up your poo-bag.'

Nelson hooked the poo-bag onto the end of his stick with a sigh, and Danny got his trainer and brolly.

'T-shirt over your head then,' Danny prompted.

They both pulled their t-shirts up, took their positions, and started the chant.

When Danny pulled his t-shirt back down after they'd finished, Nelson saw he had a big grin on his face.

'Perfect. This is going to be good. We're going to win today, I can feel it.'

Nelson didn't look convinced.

Chapter 21

'Let's go this way today Dad,' said Danny, as his Dad was about to carry on past the Hope Street turning. He was determined to go the same way they'd taken when the Crabs had beaten Stimport.

'Okay, if you want,' said Dad, turning into Hope Street instead.

Danny was pleased with the way things were going. So far, so good. He'd made sure he'd had the same breakfast and was wearing the same clothes, and Nelson had done the same. They'd done the luck-dance, together, properly, then had the same lunch, and now they were going to Springly Park the same way as before. There were only a few more things to get right now and everything would be just as it had been for the Stimport game. He had to concentrate though. He couldn't afford to get it wrong now.

They reached the stadium, and Danny led the way through the crowds milling around outside, making a beeline for the programme selling lady with the bobble hat.

'Three points today?' she asked as Dad bought one from her, making Danny smile.

'Let's hope so,' said Dad, wiping the smile off Danny's face. That wasn't right.

'Can't settle for anything less,' Danny added quickly.

Dad gave him a funny look, surprised that he'd chipped into the conversation. He thought nothing more of it though, and they carried on, through the turnstiles and into the ground.

Dad looked at his watch.

'Shall we go straight up?' he asked.

'You said you needed the toilet didn't you, Nelson?' said Danny, giving his friend a nudge.

'Did I?' said Nelson.

'Yes,' said Danny firmly.

'I didn't hear him,' said Dad, frowning, whilst Danny gave Nelson a look intended to remind him why he really needed to go to the toilet.

'Oh yeah, I might have done,' said Nelson, finally getting it and wandering off to the gents.

'Are you alright?' Dad asked Danny as they waited for Nelson.

'Yeah, fine,' said Danny.

Dad looked at him like he didn't believe him, but left it at that.

Soon, Nelson was back with them, they were in their seats and the match was kicking off.

The Crabs started strongly but were nearly caught out when the Finbury Rovers striker was put through one-on-one with Mortensen in the Chadmouth goal. The crowd held its breath, but was relieved to see the ball bounce harmlessly past the post.

'Phew, that was a let-off,' said Dad.

'It was, wasn't it,' agreed Danny, giving Nelson a knowing look.

Minutes later Finbury were made to pay for their mistake. Speirs brought the ball out from the back and passed it forward to Logan, who played a neat one-two with Sanchez before running on into the box. As a challenge came in he hit a shot. It should have been easy for the Finbury goalie, who got both hands to the ball, but it slipped through his fingers and into the net.

Danny and Nelson exchanged another glance as the crowd celebrated. It looked like their luck was in again.

With the crowd right behind them and their confidence up, Chadmouth began to play with a belief they hadn't shown all season, passing the ball around and looking dangerous going forward. They still looked a little shaky at the back though, and with a narrow one-goal lead no one was able to relax just yet.

A big cheer greeted the half-time whistle, and an even bigger one welcomed the home side back onto the pitch after the break.

Chapter 22

It took the Crabs a while to get going again, but they continued to dominate. They weren't able to create any clear-cut chances though, and the score stayed 1-0 as the second half ticked onwards.

'We could do with a second,' said Danny.

'And a third as well, the number of late goals we've had recently,' said Dad.

They had to wait until the eightieth minute before there was another goal though. Wilson made a great run down the right-wing, beating his man and racing down the touchline. He was about to cross the ball into the box when the Finbury defender, trying to recover, clipped his heel and brought him down. The crowd howled for a free-kick, and the ref agreed.

'This is better than a corner,' said Dad, as Logan placed the ball to take the free-kick halfway between the corner flag and the Finbury penalty area. Chadmouth brought the big men up from the back, sensing that this was their chance to make the three points safe.

There was all sorts of jostling in the box as Logan hit the free-kick, aiming it towards the back post where Sagar was waiting. He managed to get above his marker and headed it back towards goal. It looked like the Finbury goalie was going to catch it though, until he suddenly tumbled to the ground. The ball seemed to hang in the air, right where the goalie had been. Everyone held their breath. Who would react first? Ferguson was the closest Chadmouth player to the ball. He took a step forward, leapt up in the air, and headed the ball into the empty goal.

As Ferguson raced away to celebrate, pursued by his ecstatic teammates and cheered by the overjoyed home supporters, the Finbury players angrily surrounded the ref.

'Was that a foul on the keeper?' Dad asked Danny.

'Don't know,' said Danny. 'Don't care.'

The ref wasn't interested in anything the Finbury players had to say. He was doing his best to wave them away to carry on the game. Eventually, they realised they weren't getting anywhere with their protests, and they reluctantly made their way back to the halfway line to restart the match.

'That's surely the three points now,' said Nelson.

'You never say that!' Dad told him in horror. Danny didn't mind though. He was confident that they were going to win now. Everything they'd done before the game had worked. Two more lucky goals meant three more precious points for Chadmouth Town.

Moments later he was proved right, as the ref brought the match to an end to another huge cheer. The Crabs had won 2-0.

---

* * *

'That's three unbeaten at home now,' said Dad as they walked home.

'Two wins and a draw,' said Danny. 'Seven points out of nine.'

'Not bad,' said Nelson. 'Think you're gonna stay up yet?'

'We're up to 22nd now,' said Danny, looking at the league table on his phone. 'Four points from safety.'

'How many games left?'

'Three,' said Dad.

'Two of them at home,' added Danny, looking at Nelson meaningfully.

'Yeah,' said Dad. 'Shame they can't all be at home. We still haven't been able to find any away form. Still, our home form might just be enough to save us, if other results go our way. We just need to keep it going for two more matches.'

Danny's dad spotted another supporter he knew, and he went over to talk to him. Danny took the opportunity to talk to Nelson without his dad hearing.

'You see. I told you it'd work if we did it properly.'

'Yeah, maybe there is something in it after all.'

'Maybe? You have to admit, we get all the luck whenever we do the luck-dance and all the rest of it.'

'I suppose.'

'We just need to keep doing it right for two more matches and we might just stay up. You can come to the last two games, can't you?'

'Ah, yeah, about that.'

'What?'

'Well, you know how I had to miss the last match because of the wedding fitting?'

'Yeah. Don't tell me you've got another one.'

'Not another fitting. Just the wedding.'

'What? No. When?'

'The second of May.'

'The second of May?'

'Yeah.'

'But that's the last game of the season, against Beddingley City. It might all come down to that match. You can't miss it.'

'I can't miss my sister's wedding can I?'

'You'll have to.'

'How?'

'I dunno. We'll just have to think of something.'

'I can tell you now, my parents will never let me miss my sister's wedding.'

'Can it be moved to a different day?'

'Oh yeah, right. They've been planning it for more than a year, all the family's booked to fly over from Jamaica for it, but yeah, I'm sure they'll change it just because my mate's football team has a match that day.'

'What time is it then? Can't you just go along for the main bit then come to the match?'

'You don't understand. These things last all day in our family. I can't just leave halfway through.'

'Nelson!'

'I know. There's nothing I can do about it though. Won't your Gran be better and wanting her season ticket back by then anyway?'

'Maybe. Not sure. We can always buy you another ticket if she is.'

'Well, it doesn't matter anyway. I won't be allowed to go.'

'You have to Nelson,' said Danny desperately. 'You have to. I'll think of something.'

Chadmouth Town 2-0 Finbury Rovers
Estonpark Borough 2-3 Beddingley City
Kenton Athletic 0-2 Northford
Plumborough Town 0-2 Potterton United
Sturton Town 0-0 Marshfield County

		Played	Won	Drawn	Lost	GD	Points
19	Beddingley	43	9	12	22	-18	39
20	Finbury	43	10	8	25	-25	38
21	Plumborough	43	7	15	21	-29	36
22	Chadmouth	43	7	13	23	-33	34
23	Kenton	43	6	14	23	-32	32
24	Marshfield	43	5	15	23	-36	30

Chapter 23

It was the morning of the next game, Chadmouth versus Pottsworth United. It was going to be a tough match, as Pottsworth were on the verge of winning promotion to the Championship. Danny was hoping they'd take their foot off the gas a bit as they only needed a couple more points to be guaranteed automatic promotion. He'd also worked out that their away form wasn't as good as their home record, so he was quietly confident, especially because Nelson was coming again, as Gran still didn't feel up to going to the match. That meant they'd be able to keep their match-day routine exactly the same.

Nelson came round before lunch, and Danny was pleased to see that he had all the right clothes on and was able to confirm that he'd had beans on toast for breakfast, just as Danny had had his Weetabix. They grabbed the bag from the shed, carefully, and headed off to the park. This time though, when they got there, they weren't alone. Some kids from the year below them at school were there, about half a dozen of them, playing football. They weren't right where Danny and Nelson did their luck dance, they were about a hundred metres away, on the other side of the field, but they'd still be able to see exactly what they were doing.

'Can we wait until they've gone?' asked Nelson.

'We don't know how long they'll be.'

'We could ask them.'

'But then they'd wonder why, and they'd probably hang around just to see why we want the whole park to ourselves.'

'Well, we'll just have to wait then. I'm not doing it while they're here.'

'We might miss the match then though.'

'I don't care. It's too embarrassing.'

'Nelson! We can't miss the match. And we have to do the luck dance. Chadmouth won't win unless we do.'

'I'm sorry, you're going to have to do it on your own again.'

'But it doesn't work properly when I do it on my own.'

'Well, can't we change it a bit or something, so it's less embarrassing?'

'No. It has to be the same. You know it does.'

'Don't make me do it, Danny. You know what it'll be like for us if this gets back to school.'

'Sorry Nelson, we've got to. We can make something up if anyone asks us what we were doing.'

'Yeah? Like what?'

'I don't know. We'll think of something.'

Danny emptied the bag out onto the ground and handed Nelson his stick and poo-bag. It just made Nelson even less keen to do the luck dance.

'No way. I'm not dancing around with a bagful of dog poo when there are kids from our school just over there.'

'They probably won't even notice us. They're too busy with their

n Nelson. You can't let me down now.'

out a huge sigh.

'You know Danny, you're going to owe me *forever* after this.'

'Yeah, that's fine. Now, let's just get on with it.'

'And we're doing it quietly alright, so hopefully they won't hear us. I'm sure it'll still work, if it's going to work at all.'

'Okay, whatever. Now come on.'

Danny took his place, ready to start the luck dance, and Nelson reluctantly followed suit. Danny started the chant, not too loudly, as Nelson had requested.

'Fi.'

'Fi.'

'Fi fie.'

'Fi fie.'

'Fi fie fo.'

Nelson suddenly stopped what they were doing, looking over to the kids playing football.

'They're watching us, Danny. Oh, why did I ever come up with this?'

Danny looked round too.

'No they're not. You're imagining it. Come on. Keep going.'

'Fi fie fo.'

'Kumala.'

'Kumala.'

'Vista.'

'Vista.'

'Kumala kumala kumala vista.'

'Kumala kumala kumala vista.'

'Oh la-noh la-noh la-vista.'

'Not so loud. You're getting louder,' complained Nelson.

'Sorry,' said Danny, before repeating his line more quietly.

'Oh la-noh la-noh la-vista.'

'Oh la-noh la-noh la-vista.'

'Eenie meenie dessameenie ooh-aah ooh-orrameenie.'

'Eenie meenie dessameenie ooh-aah ooh-orrameenie.'

'Beep deedly oden boden bodash skadutendaten.'

'Beep deedly oden boden bodash skadutendaten.'

Nelson took an anxious look over to the other kids, to check whether they'd noticed their strange antics. He wasn't sure if they had or not. He *really* hoped they hadn't.

Chapter 24

When they got back Danny's mum asked them what they wanted for lunch.

'Cheese rolls and pickled onion Monster Munch please,' said Danny without hesitation.

'Again?' said Mum. 'That's all you seem to eat on Saturdays these days. How about you Nelson?'

'Same for me please,' said Nelson. He knew the drill by now.

'Right, well, two cheese rolls and pickled onion Monster Munch coming up. You can be washing your hands ready.'

She started making their rolls whilst the two boys did as they were told. She placed their rolls on the table and started rummaging in the cupboard for the crisps.

'Oh, it doesn't look like we've got any Monster Munch I'm afraid. It'll have to be Hula-Hoops instead.'

'What?' said Danny in a panic. 'Are you sure?'

Mum had another rummage.

'No, there's definitely no Monster Munch.'

Danny looked at Nelson in alarm.

'This is terrible.'

'They're only crisps,' said Mum, looking confused. 'I thought you liked Hula-Hoops.'

'Oh, yeah I do. But…er, Nelson doesn't, do you, Nelson?'

'Me? Oh, no. Hate them. Too, um, hoopy.'

'Oh, well, in that case, you can go to the corner shop to get some if you want to.'

'Thanks, Mum. Come on Nelson.'

'You'd better be quick though,' she added. 'You don't want to be late leaving for the match.'

She gave Danny some money and the two boys put their trainers back on before jogging round to the corner shop. Danny was cross with himself for not checking that they had all the right food in the house. What if they hadn't had cheese or rolls either, or Weetabix? He was pretty sure they didn't sell any of those things at the corner shop. It could have been a disaster. It still could be if the corner shop was out of pickled onion Monster Munch.

It was alright though - the shop had plenty of pickled onion Monster, Munch. He was very relieved, and told himself he would have to check they had everything they needed before the next game.

'I've got a confession,' said Nelson as they waited to pay behind an elderly lady who was deep in conversation with the shopkeeper about how terrible the bus service had been lately.

'What's that?' asked Danny.

'That last match, the one we won 2-0.'

'Yeah?'

'When we did the luck dance beforehand.'

'Yeah?'

'And we did everything the same, like what we ate, what we wore…'

'Yeah?'

Nelson paused before he carried on, looking sheepish.

'I had different underpants on.'

'You what?!' hissed Danny.

'I knew I shouldn't tell you. I knew you'd be like this.'

'Like what? Like what? Your pants could have ruined our season. You could have got us relegated.'

'But I didn't though did I? We still won didn't we?'

'Well, yeah. But you didn't know we would. I can't believe you took a risk like that. It's alright for you, glory-hunting, Premier League supporters, but this is life or death to us.'

'Don't call me a glory-hunter. I want Chadmouth to stay up as much as you do.' Danny frowned at him.

'Well, maybe not quite as much, but I do want them to stay up.'

'I can't believe you took that risk though.'

'I didn't have any choice. I was able to get my dirty t-shirt out of the wash basket when I went home to change, but Dad had put my pants in the wash and they were still soaking. You can't force me to wear wet pants.'

The lady in front of them and the shopkeeper paused their conversation and gave the boys very funny looks. They lowered their voices.

'Let's just...' began Nelson. 'Can we stop talking about my pants, please?'

'Yeah, I think we should.'

The lady had finally finished chatting and left the shop, and Danny put the two packets of crisps on the counter.

'The point is,' said Nelson, 'this proves that we don't have to do everything exactly the same all day long for it to work.'

'Well, maybe, but how do we know which bits we have to do and which bits we don't?'

The shopkeeper handed Danny his change. Danny grabbed their crisps, and they left the shop.

'Well, we don't I suppose...'

'...until it's too late. We haven't got points to play with. We can't risk losing, or even drawing anymore.'

'But we might not have a choice. If I can't get out of going to this wedding I won't be able to come to the Beddingley match. I can have the same thing for breakfast, and maybe lunch as well if I take it with me, and I might be able to find somewhere private where I can quietly do the luck dance on my own, but that'll be about it. I won't even be able to wear the right clothes.'

'You could wear the right pants… for a change.'

'Okay, okay. I could wear my pants, and socks, if I can make sure they're clean and dry. I've got them on today, by the way, the ones I wore for Stimport, you'll be pleased to hear.'

'Good. I don't like it though, about missing the last match.'

'Neither do I. But I don't think we've got any choice.'

'We'll just have to think of something.'

They ran back home, ate their lunch, including their newly purchased crisps, said thanks to Danny's mum again, and went to see if his dad was ready.

Chapter 25

Halfway to the ground, they faced another problem.

'I don't see why you never want to go down Church Street any more,' said Dad as the three of them stood at the junction of Station Road and Hope Street again.

'I just don't,' said Danny, who still wasn't ready to tell Dad about his match day routine after their conversation about superstitions. He'd also warned Nelson not to mention it, as his dad would only laugh at them. It might have been easier to tell him, let him make fun of them, then get on with it, but he just didn't want to.

'But why though? Is there something down there you don't want to see or something? Has something happened?'

'No, nothing's happened. I just… prefer going down Hope Street. That's all.'

'But we've gone that way the last few times now. We always used to mix it up a bit,' argued Dad.

'Yeah, well, maybe this way's quicker.'

'It's not quicker. They're both exactly the same.'

'It does *seem* quicker,' said Nelson, trying his best to help Danny out.

'But it's not,' insisted Dad. 'Is it because Hope Street's called Hope Street. It gives you hope or something?'

'Well, why are you so keen *not* to go down Hope Street?' asked Danny instead of answering him. 'Is there something down there that *you* don't want to see?'

Dad sighed impatiently, but to Danny and Nelson's relief started walking down Hope Street, shaking his head.

'Oh, whatever.'

They walked the rest of the way to the ground in silence. Why were they finding it so hard to follow the routine today? First, there had been other kids at the park when they'd done the luck dance, then they'd run out of pickled onion Monster Munch, and now Dad was making a fuss about which way they walked to the stadium. He hoped the remaining bits of the routine would go a bit more smoothly.

They didn't though. Dad bought a programme from the usual seller, which was good, but, perhaps sensing that he was in a strop, the seller didn't say anything to him. Danny started to panic. That could be the crucial bit. The rest of their efforts could have been completely in vain if they didn't finish the routine off properly. He was going to have to do it himself.

'Three points today? Can't settle for anything less,' he blurted out.

The programme seller and Dad but both looked at him like he was completely mad.

'Are you taking the…' the programme seller started to say.

'What's got into you today?' asked Dad.

'Come on,' said Nelson, coming to Danny's rescue. 'Kick-off's in a minute.'

The programme seller gave Danny a dirty look, and Dad seemed only too happy to follow Nelson's lead and head into the ground.

That just left one more thing for them to do, but that was a problem too. Nelson went off for a wee, as he always did, but Danny was bursting for one too. He really, really needed to go because he'd forgotten to go before they left the house as he was flustered about the crisps and Nelson's pants. He was determined not to go now though. He tried not to jiggle about too much as he waited, enviously, for Nelson to finish. He didn't want Dad spotting that he was desperate and making him go.

It seemed to take ages for the match to begin, as he sat in his seat, trying his best not to wet himself. He was sure that as long as he waited for the match to start before he went that wouldn't spoil the routine. Finally, kick-off came, and he jumped up and ran to the toilet as quickly as he could as soon as it did.

'Is he alright?' Dad asked Nelson as Danny raced off.

'Yeah, I think so,' said Nelson. 'Just nervous I think.'

Dad seemed to accept that explanation, and Danny was soon back in his seat, having not missed much at all.

There wasn't much to see when he did get back either. Chadmouth were looking nervous, despite being unbeaten in their last three matches. Maybe they were now starting to believe they could escape relegation and were scared of making a mistake and spoiling it. They looked uncomfortable on the ball and were giving it away too easily. Their opponents, Pottsworth United were, in contrast passing the ball around nicely, looking every bit a team on the brink of promotion. They always seemed to have a team-mate to pass to, although they didn't always make much progress forward when they did, and they hadn't threatened the Chadmouth goal yet.

'I'd love to see the possession stats,' said Danny to Nelson.

'About 90% Pottsworth I reckon,' agreed Nelson.

'No shots on target though,' added Dad. 'That'll do me. We'll get it together in a minute.'

The crowd seemed a bit out of sorts today as well as the players, thought Danny. It was the kind of game that just needed something to spark it into life. The men who sat behind them had clearly lost interest in the match, and were debating whether Chadmouth should switch to a 5-4-1 formation, which they may or may not have used when they beat either Blueport City or possibly Sturton Town, 5-0 or maybe 6-1, in 2007 or 2008, depending on which one of them you believed.

Unfortunately, the first real action of the game came in the Chadmouth penalty area. Towards the end of the half, Pottsworth put together another tidy passing move, working the ball down their left-hand side with some quick, first-time balls. Their captain dummied and cut into the Chadmouth box then laid the ball off to a teammate who was about to shoot. He never got the chance though, as Duffy lunged in with a desperate challenge, missed the ball completely and took out the Pottsworth attacker instead. The crowd groaned as the referee pointed to the penalty spot, but nobody had any complaints. It was as clear-cut a penalty as you would ever see.

Danny looked anxiously at Nelson. This wasn't supposed to happen. What had they done wrong? He was sure they'd done everything right, even though it hadn't been easy.

Chapter 26

Pottsworth's captain was going to take the spot kick himself. The Chadmouth fans behind the goal were doing their best to put him off, jumping around and waving their arms and scarves around. Boos and whistles rang out around the ground as the Pottsworth player started his long run-up. He sprinted up to the ball, gave it an almighty boot, and sent it flying straight over the bar into the Chadmouth fans. The boos and whistles were instantly replaced by cheers and jeers, as the penalty taker put his head in his hands. The Crabs had been let off the hook. Danny felt a bit better now. Maybe they *had* got everything right today, and their luck was in again.

That was as exciting as the first half got, and everyone was hoping for more action in the second half. Wedlock had made one change during the break, bringing on Watson for Parker, and it seemed to make an instant difference, with the young academy player making a couple of attacking runs that got the crowd going. The rest of the team started playing with more urgency and confidence too, and they soon had Pottsworth on the back foot. A dangerous cross by Wilson almost found Ferguson in the box, and a long-range effort by Sanchez produced a good save.

'We need to turn this pressure into a goal before Pottsworth get back into it,' said Dad.

Danny just nodded. He was too nervous to speak.

It looked like it wasn't going to happen though. The Crabs continued to dominate the second half, but couldn't find a goal. Ferguson just failed to latch onto a through ball that would have put him one-on-one with the goalie, and a dangerous, whipped in corner was flicked on by Speirs at the near-post but was just too high for Burbanks at the back.

'It's not going to happen is it,' said Dad in frustration. 'It's not going to happen.'

But he was wrong. With a quarter of an hour left on the clock, and Pottsworth doing their best to take the sting out of the match by keeping possession, one of the Pottsworth defenders tried a back-pass to his goalie. His pass was much too short though, and Watson, the young substitute, was on it in a flash. His first touch was perfect, taking the ball around the goalkeeper, who slipped as he tried to turn. With the keeper on his backside and the defenders struggling to get back, he calmly looked up, picked his spot, and slotted the ball into the empty net.

The crowd went wild. Watson was mobbed by his teammates as he celebrated in front of the Chadmouth faithful, and there was another massive cheer when the announcer confirmed the name of the goal-scorer. He was one of their own, a local lad who'd joined their academy as a boy, which made it even sweeter for the fans. Mind you, thought Danny as he and everyone else finally sat back down, the goal could have been scored by his mum or Mrs Kaur – if it meant three points for Chadmouth it made no difference at all who scored it.

Now all they had to do was keep a clean sheet to hold on to their lead.

Chapter 27

Chadmouth had not been good at holding onto leads that season though, and Pottsworth, anxious for at least a point to help their promotion charge, seemed to have decided that it was time to be a bit more attacking in their play.

The Crabs also seemed unsure whether to go for a second goal to wrap up the three points or defend what they had. Gradually, they were being pushed further and further into their own half.

'They're sitting too deep, they're sitting too deep,' grumbled Danny.

'Push out, push out!' shouted Dad, frantically waving his hands around as if he could actually move them himself.

Now Chadmouth really did seem nervous, and the crowd were too every time the visitors got the ball anywhere near the Crabs' penalty area. It was going to be a very long last five minutes. The clock slowly ticked down to four minutes, then three. Danny kept checking the time on his phone, so at least Dad was spared having to tell Danny how long was left all the time.

Two minutes to go, then one minute, then… disaster. Pottsworth mounted another attack, which was snuffed out by a well-timed tackle by Duffy at the expense of a throw-in. They took it quickly, before the tiring Chadmouth defence had regrouped, and their captain was clear on their right-wing. He looked up, saw a team-mate racing into the box and produced an inch-perfect pass right into his path, and the ball was slotted neatly into the bottom corner to make it 1-1. Springly Park fell silent as the Pottsworth players celebrated. Had that just sealed their fate? Were they going down now?

'Hang on,' said Nelson though. 'Look at the linesman.'

Danny and his Dad looked, as did the rest of the crowd. The linesman had his flag up, and was waving it to get the referee's attention. The ref spotted his assistant and jogged over to see what he wanted.

'Offside? Was it offside?' said Danny excitedly.

The whole stadium held its breath. This was a huge decision. It could decide the outcome of their whole season. It seemed to take ages, but finally the referee reached a decision. He blew his whistle and waved his arms to indicate that the goal was disallowed.

'No goal!' shouted Danny, Dad, Nelson and almost everyone around them in delight.

'Was it really offside though?' asked Danny again.

'I don't think so, but I don't care,' answered Dad.

Chadmouth had had an enormous slice of luck again. The Pottsworth players were not so happy about it, and nor was their manager, who raced over to the linesman to protest. The decision stood though, and Chadmouth were still 1-0 up.

And that's how the match ended a minute or so later.

'Where are we in the league now then,' Nelson asked Danny, who as always had all the relevant information to hand, as they walked home with big smiles on their faces.

'Up to 21st,' he answered, 'and we're only three points from safety now.'

'With two games to go,' added Dad.

'But one of those is away,' said Danny miserably.

'That's alright,' said Dad brightly. 'We've got a bit of momentum now.'

Danny looked at Nelson. They both knew the difference between home and away matches, and the likelihood of Chadmouth winning them.

Chadmouth Town 1-0 Pottsworth United
Estonpark Borough 0-0 Beddingley City
Fishton Grove 1-1 Marshfield County
Kenton Athletic 2-0 Greaseworth City
Plumborough Town 1-2 Libley United
Sturton Town 1-2 Finbury Rovers

		Played	Won	Drawn	Lost	GD	Points
19	Finbury	44	11	8	25	-24	41
20	Beddingley	44	9	13	22	-18	40
21	Chadmouth	44	8	13	23	-32	37
22	Plumborough	44	7	15	22	-30	36
23	Kenton	44	7	14	23	-30	35
24	Marshfield	44	5	16	23	-36	31

Chapter 28

Danny was on top of the world for the rest of the weekend, and still was when he set off for school on Monday morning. That wasn't about to last for long though.

'Hey, it's the freaks!' shouted Ashton, as Danny and Nelson walked into school at the start of the day.

'Just when you thought Danny Mann Pants Team Fan couldn't get any weirder,' jeered Louis.

'So, what were you doing in the park on Saturday then, Mann?' asked Ashton. 'We heard about your little dance, waving sticks around and crawling around on your knees.'

'Praying for a miracle to save your rubbish team?' suggested Jackson.

'How does it go?' taunted Taylor, marching round and round in a circle waving her arms around madly in the air. The rest of the Prem Gang joined in, making ridiculous noises and laughing.

'Oh, hang on,' sniggered Louis, 'we've forgotten our twigs.'

They all laughed even louder at that. Danny badly wanted to hit them to shut them up, but he remembered his conversation with Mr Quibley. There was no way he was going to risk missing any Chadmouth matches because of Ashton and his stupid mates.

'Come on Nelson,' he said through gritted teeth, 'let's ignore these idiots.'

Danny and Nelson tried to ignore them and walk on past, but Ashton and the others followed them.

'What are you doing hanging around with that loser, Nelson?'

'He's infected you with his weirdness.'

'And his terrible taste in football teams.'

'Are you a loser Chadmouth supporter as well now Nelson?'

'My dad says they're going to go bust if they go down. Then they won't even exist anymore.'

'Good!'

'Then you'll have to find a *real* team to support Mann.'

Danny stopped. He'd had enough now.

'Shut your mouths!' he shouted at them. 'You know nothing. You all think you know about football but you haven't got a clue. You'll never understand what *real* football is all about, as long as you're plastic, glory-hunters.'

Ashton, Taylor, Jackson and Louis just laughed at his outburst and started to do their version of the luck-dance again. Danny started towards them, clenching his fists, but Nelson grabbed him and pulled him away.

'No Danny. Don't bother. You know it'll be you that gets into trouble.'

Danny glared at them, but slowly started to calm down. He and Nelson started walking away again, and this time the Prem Gang, still laughing, let them go. The two boys found a quiet spot away from anyone else.

'I told you those kids at the park could see us,' moaned Nelson.

'I'm sorry,' said Danny, 'but we had to do it.'

'No, we didn't.'

'Yes we did. Chadmouth wouldn't have won if we hadn't. You saw what happened, that missed penalty, our goal from that terrible back-pass, their equaliser ruled out for offside.'

'Danny, those things happen in football all the time.'

'Not to us they don't. Not this season.'

'If you've had bad luck all season it's probably just your turn to have a bit of good luck then.'

'You sound like my dad. That's what he thinks is happening.'

'There you go then. It wasn't because of us. It couldn't have been because of us. We haven't got super powers or anything.'

'It *was* because of us. Every time we do it all properly we're really lucky. Every time we don't, we aren't.'

'You can believe it if you want, but I don't. I'm not going to do it anymore. It's too embarrassing. You're too embarrassing.'

'You can't say that.'

'I just did. I can't come to the last game anyway, so it makes no difference.'

'Nelson…'

'No Danny. I'm not coming. I'm going to my sister's wedding and that's that. I never want to see another Chadmouth Town match as long as I live, and I'm certainly not doing any stupid dance beforehand, or eating and wearing what you tell me to.'

The bell rang for the start of school, and Nelson stomped off, leaving Danny behind.

'Nelson.'

But Nelson just ignored him.

* * *

As soon as he got home later, Danny went online. He'd been worrying about what Ashton had said about Chadmouth going bust if they got relegated. He was hoping it wasn't true, but he soon found out that it was. He found an article on the local paper's website that said that the club was already in trouble, with debts mounting up. If they got relegated they'd get even less money than they did now. They could sell some players, but even that might not be enough. The club could actually cease to exist if they went down.

That was just great. Now he wasn't just responsible for making sure the Crabs stayed up – it was up to him to make sure they even continued to exist!

It was more important than ever that he got Nelson to go to the match. He had no idea how he was going to do it though.

Chapter 29

Danny was very relieved to get to the end of the next school day. He'd had one of the worst days he could remember. The Prem Gang had barely stopped teasing him, and Nelson was still refusing to speak to him. He was also feeling miserable because The Crabs were doomed to go down if he couldn't get Nelson to change his mind, *and* somehow find a way for him to miss the wedding. It didn't look good.

Maybe life would be easier if he supported a big team. It wasn't going to happen though. Real football fans couldn't just change their minds about who they supported. If you support a team, you support them for life.

When Dad got home from work they went to visit Gran, who was out of hospital and back home now (without Danny having to smuggle her out), which was good news at least. She seemed a bit better now, and she wasn't coughing as much. She noticed that her grandson didn't look very happy though.

'What's the matter with you?' she asked him. 'You look like you've lost a pound and found a penny.'

'I'm just worried about Chadmouth,' Danny told her, without going into detail about why.

'There's no point in worrying about it Danny,' she said. 'You can't do anything about it. It's all out of your hands.'

Danny thought about telling her that it was very much *in* his hands, but he didn't whilst his dad was there. He'd made it clear the other night what he thought about "superstidiots".

'Do you think you'll be well enough to go?' he asked her instead.

'We'll have to wait and see,' she answered with a smile.

'I don't think that's a good idea,' said Dad. 'You've only just got back from the hospital, and you heard what the doctor said. You need to take it easy.'

'Oh, I'm alright. I'm a tough old goat,' laughed Gran.

'Even so,' said Dad.

'I'd like to see you try to stop me. It'll be our most important match for years.'

'As long as we get a result at Throckmorton and Beddingley don't win tomorrow night,' pointed out Danny.

'Oh, I think we will,' said Gran. 'We're on a good run of form now.'

'Only when we…' Danny started to say. He had been about to say that their form was only good when he and Nelson did the luck-dance and they followed the rest of the routine, before he stopped himself.

'Only when we what?' asked Dad.

'Er, only when we're home,' said Danny quickly. 'Our away form is still rubbish.'

'That's true,' agreed Gran. 'I still think it'll be all to play for on Saturday though.'

'And you'll be right here, listening to it on the radio,' said Dad.

'Hmm. We'll see,' grumbled Gran.

Dad left them to it and went into the kitchen to put away some shopping they'd picked up for Gran on the way.

'Has your friend been enjoying the matches?' asked Gran. 'The one who's been borrowing my ticket.'

'I think so,' said Danny. 'He's a Liverpool fan really, but I think he's getting into Chadmouth a bit now.' He didn't mention that Nelson wasn't actually speaking to him anymore after the row they'd had.

'Are you taking him to the Beddingley match?'

'I don't know. He's supposed to be at his sister's wedding on the same day, so I'm not sure what he's doing.'

'Ah, I see.'

Dad came out of the kitchen just then.

'We forgot the milk, Danny. I told you to remind me.'

'Oh yeah, sorry.'

'I'll just pop out and get some. You stay here and chat to Gran.'

He left the room and they heard the front door close.

'So, are we going to beat Beddingley then?' asked Gran.

'Not sure,' answered Danny glumly.

'What's the matter?' asked Gran. 'You've been so confident recently. Why the change of heart?'

Danny wondered what to say. He felt like he wanted to tell her everything that had been going on. Even though Dad would think it was stupid, he had a feeling Gran would understand. He decided to let her in on the secret.

Chapter 30

'Gran, something funny's been happening, at the matches,' said Danny.

'Funny? What do you mean?'

'Well, you know we've had some really big decisions go our way lately?'

'About time too.'

'Yeah, like, scoring goals that were actually offside and having goals against us disallowed when they should have been allowed.'

'And penalty misses, deflected goals and terrible back-passes?'

'Yeah… Well, it's all because of me.'

It sounded stupid now that he said it out loud.

'Because of you?'

'Yeah. Well, me and Nelson.'

'Go on.'

Danny took a deep breath and started telling her all about the luck-dance and everything else, like what they ate and what they wore, how they got to the stadium, what they said to the programme seller, and how only Nelson was allowed to go to the toilet before the match started.

When he finished his story he stopped, and waited for her reaction.

'That's very interesting,' she said eventually. 'Very interesting indeed.'

He waited for her to say something else, but she didn't. She just sat there, looking thoughtful.

'I thought you'd tell me how ridiculous I was being,' said Danny after a minute.

'Ridiculous? Not at all,' said Gran, with a faraway look in her eyes. 'You know, this reminds me of something.'

Danny waited expectantly, waiting for her to tell him more. After a moment she nodded to herself, and smiled.

'It's a long time ago now, back in the 1960s. We were one of the best teams in the country back then. I know, it's hard to believe isn't it, but we were. We had a brilliant young team, most of them local boys, and an inspirational manager. In those days even small clubs like Chadmouth could get to the top division, it wasn't all about money. Anyway, we were in the First Division, before it became the Premier League, fairly comfortable in mid-table, and it was time for the FA Cup to start. We were drawn against Everton in our first match, who were top of the league and unbeaten all season. I went along with my father, your great-grandad. I'd have been 12 or 13 at the time, and on the way to the ground my dad bought me a quarter of liquorice allsorts at the corner shop.'

'Urgh, I hate liquorice,' said Danny. 'Sorry,' he added when he saw the look on Gran's face for interrupting her.

'Anyway, we'd been studying poetry at school that week, and it suddenly popped into my head that "wish" was a good rhyme for "liquorice", and from nowhere I found myself saying out loud – "We'll win the game, that is my wish, and you shall have some liquorice", and I threw a sweet, one of the pink nobbly ones, in front of a car that was driving past us, so that it was squashed under one of its wheels. I've no idea why. It just seemed like the right thing to do. And we beat them! 2-0. Nobody could believe it. We were drawn at home in the next round as well, and I made sure we bought a quarter of liquorice allsorts on the way again. I said my rhyme and threw the sweet...'

'A pink nobbly one?'

'A pink nobbly one, and we won again. In the next round we were away, and only drew, but we won the replay at home and, yes, I did it all again on the way there. Anyway, we eventually got to the final, at Wembley, and we managed to get tickets. I took my liquorice, said my rhyme and threw a pink nobbly liquorice under a car outside the stadium, and we beat Manchester United in the final to win the cup. It was incredible Danny, I wish you could have been there.'

'So do I,' nodded Danny.

'But anyway, what I'm saying is, I don't think we'd have won the FA Cup if I hadn't said my rhyme and thrown my sweet on the way to the match every time. Don't ask me why, but somehow, it seemed to work. You've obviously stumbled across something similar. It doesn't matter why it works, you've just got to keep doing it.'

'I will Gran, I will,' said Danny.

'Good boy, good boy,' Gran smiled.

'Do you think we'll ever be that good again?' asked Danny. Gran smiled.

'When you support a small team Danny, you keep holding on to a tiny bit of hope that eventually, one day, your team could reach the top, taking on the big boys in the Premier League every week. But really, deep down, you know it's not possible, not like it was in the 60s. You need millions to get to the Premier League these days, and that's something we haven't got. Don't ever stop dreaming though Danny.'

Just then Dad returned with the milk, catching the end of their conversation.

'What are we dreaming about now?' he asked.

'Oh, just getting to the Premier League and winning the FA Cup,' Gran told him.

'Oh, right. Well, I'd settle for not getting relegated from League One at the moment,' he chuckled.

He went off to put the milk in the fridge, and Danny followed him into the kitchen to get himself a drink. Gran looked thoughtful again.

'I wonder,' she said to herself. 'I wonder.'

Chapter 31

The following evening, after another horrible school day full of teasing and Nelson still not speaking to him, Danny and his dad switched on the radio and sat down together to listen to Chadmouth's last-but-one game, away at Throckmorton Town. Danny was also following the live coverage online on his phone, so he could keep an eye on how Beddingley City and Finbury Rovers, the teams just above them, were getting on. If they both won and Chadmouth didn't, that would be it. The Crabs would be down. The tension was almost unbearable, especially as Danny always found it more nerve-wracking when he couldn't see the action. By the look of it, Dad was the same.

The night got off to the worst possible start though, when Beddingley went 1-0 up against Parkbridge United, and Finbury promptly scored to go 1-0 up in their match too. At half time Beddingley and Finbury were both still ahead, and with Chadmouth's game still goalless, that would be enough to relegate them if the scores stayed that way.

Early in the second half Finbury scored a second goal, putting them in a strong position to secure their safety. Nothing much was happening at Throckmorton, but it was all going on at Finbury, where the home side conceded a goal but quickly restored their two-goal advantage with their third of the game. It was up to the other teams to respond, with twenty minutes to go.

Danny desperately hoped that Beddingley would concede in their match, and that's exactly what happened, when Parkbridge made it 1-1. It got even better for Chadmouth a few minutes later as well, when Parkbridge scored again to put Beddingley 2-1 behind. Danny and Dad jumped up to celebrate that goal as if the Crabs had just scored. That was something that wasn't about to happen though, and their own uneventful match was the first of the night to finish, ending 0-0 and earning them a precious point.

One by one the other full-time whistles went, with Finbury securing their survival with a 3-1 victory, but Danny and his dad were happy to hear the news that Beddingley had lost 2-1. Kenton had lost and Plumborough had drawn, meaning that they were both definitely down, joining Marshfield, and leaving just one more relegation place to be filled.

'That'll do,' said Dad, sounding exhausted. 'We're still in with a chance on Saturday. It's between us and Beddingley. If we beat them, we stay up, if not then we go down and they survive.'

Danny could hardly reply. He was completely drained from the tension. What on earth was it going to be like on Saturday?

Allerborough United 2-0 Kenton Athletic
Beddingley City 1-2 Parkbridge United
Finbury Rovers 3-1 Greasworth City
Marshfield County 1-1 Blueport City
Northford 1-0 Plumborough Town
Throckmorton Town 0-0 Chadmouth Town

		Played	Won	Drawn	Lost	GD	Points
19	Finbury	45	12	8	25	-22	44
20	Beddingley	45	9	13	23	-19	40
21	Chadmouth	45	8	14	23	-32	38
22	Plumborough	45	7	15	23	-31	36
23	Kenton	45	7	14	24	-32	35
24	Marshfield	45	5	17	23	-36	32

Chapter 32

Danny was a bit happier going to school the next day. He'd received a message from Nelson after the previous night's results saying:

OK DRAW, AND BEDDINGLEY RESULT GOOD TOO. HOPE WE CAN DO IT ON SATURDAY! ☺

Danny took it as a sign that Nelson wasn't cross with him anymore, and he was proved right when Nelson arrived in the playground.

'Alright,' said Nelson.

'Alright.'

'Decent results last night.'

'Yeah. Just enough to keep us in with a chance.'

'Fingers crossed we stay up.'

It was going to take more than a few crossed fingers, thought Danny, but he wasn't going to push Nelson on that just after they'd made up again.

Nelson had brought a football in with him, and they passed it to each other in silence for a few minutes. Fortunately, the Prem Gang were too wrapped up in their own game to notice them.

'You said "we",' said Danny thoughtfully after a while.

'What?'

'When you talk about Chadmouth. You've started saying "we" and "us" instead of "you".'

'Yeah, well…'

'Does that mean you're a Chadmouth Town supporter now instead of Liverpool?'

'No. I still like Liverpool, but I like Chadmouth too. Chadmouth are, like, my second team now.'

'Okay. Cool. So, you'd still support Liverpool if they played each other then?'

'It's not likely to happen, is it? I mean, unless Chadmouth have a cup-run I suppose. But they're in different leagues, and Chadmouth aren't ever likely to get into the Premier League are they?'

There was an awkward silence. Danny didn't want to fall out with Nelson again, but he didn't want to think that his team would *never* make it to the top league. Never stop dreaming, as Gran had told him.

'Sorry,' said Nelson, realising he'd said the wrong thing. 'I didn't mean... I mean... it would be great if they did, but...'

'It's Okay,' said Danny. Like Gran had said, it was unlikely unless a multi-millionaire decided to buy the club. 'You're right. It'll probably never happen.'

'Anyway, can you imagine what my dad would say if I told him I wasn't supporting Liverpool anymore?'

'Something about being there when Liverpool won the Champions League in Istanbul?'

'Well, yeah, that too, but mainly he'd disown me.'

'Yeah, true.'

'I asked my parents again if I could go to the match on Saturday by the way,' said Nelson.

'What did they say?'

'Still no. So I asked my sister, but she said no as well.'

'So, I'm going to have to go to the match we absolutely have to win without us sticking to the routine then?'

'Looks like it. Sorry. They might still win. They might be a bit more confident now, having won a few. That might help.'

'Maybe,' said Danny, not convinced.

'I would do it, you know,' said Nelson. 'The luck dance and the rest of it. If I could.'

'I know,' said Danny. 'Thanks.'

Danny was in a good mood, as he was friends with Nelson again, even though he hadn't thought of a way to get Nelson to the crucial match. His good mood wasn't going to last for long though.

Chapter 33

'Scraped a draw last night then,' smirked Ashton, as he and his three friends barged their way past some other kids in the playground to confront Danny and Nelson. 'Won't do you any good though. You're going down anyway.'

'Looks like you've been following our results,' Danny replied. 'Want to come along on Saturday?'

Ashton and the others made a big deal of laughing at this.

'Get ready for life in League Two,' sneered Taylor.

'But don't get too used to it,' added Jackson. 'You'll be getting relegated again next season.'

'If you don't go bust first!'

'You seem to know a lot about it. Fans of lower league football are you?' Danny responded, knowing that would wind them up further.

'You're joking aren't you?' spluttered Ashton. 'As if we'd be interested in the rubbish *you* call football.'

'Yeah,' added Louis. 'If it's not in the Premier League, it's not football.'

'Oh, so the Champion League's not football is it, or La Liga, or Serie A?' snapped Danny.

'Danny,' warned Nelson, not wanting his friend not to wind them up too much.

'Shut up Mann, you know what he meant,' snarled Ashton.

Danny took a deep breath. He could see where this was going, but he wasn't going to let it. It was boring him now, arguing about which was better out of Premier League or lower league football almost every day.

'Look,' he began. 'I can't be bothered to argue about this with you anymore. You all support big teams, and I support a small team. You don't understand what it's like for me, and maybe I don't understand what it's like for you. That's just the way it is. I know how much I love my club, and I don't care what you think about that. And you can support whoever you want, I really don't care.'

Ashton, Jackson, Taylor and Louis were just listening to him, as was Nelson, who was surprised that Danny hadn't just taken the bait and done something he regretted.

'So from now on,' he continued, 'you can say whatever you want about Chadmouth Town, and I'll just ignore you. And I'll stop having a go at you and your teams as well. I love football, and you love football, and arguing about it is just a waste of time.'

With that, Danny just walked away from the Prem Gang to the other side of the playground, followed by an open-mouthed Nelson. The Prem Gang also seemed shocked by his little speech, and just watched him go.

A bit further along the playground, unseen by Danny, Mr Quibley quietly closed his office window and smiled to himself. He'd heard everything Danny had just said and was very happy to hear that, for once, someone had listened to his advice.

Chapter 34

'And I'm telling you, I'm feeling much better now,' insisted Gran. Danny and his dad were visiting Gran again, with just two days to go before the big match.

'You're still not in any fit state to sit in a cold football stadium for two hours, especially with the kind of stress that there's going to be on Saturday,' insisted Dad.

'Oh, it's not going to be cold – the weather's lovely at the moment – and anyway, I'm going to be stressed whether I'm there watching or here listening to the radio.'

'I find it worse listening on the radio, to be honest,' chipped in Danny, and got a glare from his Dad.

'I still think it's best for you if you don't go,' said Dad. 'I'm only thinking of you.'

'Well I'm seventy years old and I've had plenty of practice of thinking for myself thank you very much.'

'Oh, I give up,' grumbled Dad. 'I'm going to make a drink. Who wants a cup of tea?'

'I don't know,' said Gran with a mischievous smile. 'Am I allowed one?'

'Grrrnnnhhhhh!' muttered Dad, and went out to the kitchen to put the kettle on.

Gran gave Danny a satisfied smile when he'd gone.

'Do you think you will come, Gran?' Danny asked her.

'I don't know. I'll have to see how I'm feeling.'

'It's just that…'

'Nelson can come with you whether I go or not. We can always buy another ticket. It never sells out there, even when it's a big match, and that seat between us and the wall is always free isn't it.'

'I suppose,' Danny reluctantly agreed, 'although he might not be able to come anyway, like I told you.'

He wondered whether the ritual would work if four of them went to the game instead of three. They hadn't tried that yet. And would Gran be able to walk to the ground? Dad would probably want to get a taxi instead. That would mess things up big style.

'You're worried about your routine aren't you,' said Gran, reading his mind. 'Me coming along could mess it up, couldn't it?'

'Yeah,' Danny admitted. 'I'd love you to be there of course, but yeah, it might not work if you come.'

'Well,' said Gran with a sigh. 'I wouldn't want to be the one to blame for Chadmouth getting relegated. That would never do.'

She looked thoughtful for a moment before speaking again.

'I'll give it some thought,' she said eventually, as the sound of Dad stirring the drinks came from the kitchen. 'It's a big decision, isn't it?'

Danny nodded.

* * *

The following evening Gran still hadn't made her mind up whether she was going to the match or not, saying she wanted to give herself as long as she could to see how she was feeling. Danny had told Nelson he could come whether his Gran did or not. He still wondered whether it would work if she went to the game, but it wouldn't matter anyway if Nelson didn't.

Nelson still hadn't thought of a way to get out of going to the wedding, and neither had Danny. They were running out of time fast. The match was the next day. Both boys were sure that if they couldn't find a way for Nelson to get there it could be the end for Chadmouth Town.

The possibility of Nelson missing the game didn't stop Danny from making the rest of his preparations though. After the near-disasters of the previous weekend he was determined to leave nothing to chance this time. He'd checked that they had plenty of Weetabix, and had got Nelson to make sure he had everything he needed for his beans on toast. He'd also made sure they had rolls, cheese, butter and pickled onion Monster Munch, which they did, and that his Chadmouth shirt and the right jeans, pants and socks were clean. He'd also got Nelson to give him all the clothes he needed to be wearing, so he could stash them in his bedroom. It seemed safer to keep them there instead of at Nelson's house. If they could get Nelson away from the wedding it would be gutting if he then didn't have the right clothes.

Everything was ready for Saturday. Everything apart from Nelson. Danny desperately needed a plan.

Chapter 35

Danny couldn't sleep that night. He spent hours tossing and turning in bed, worrying about the match and everything he needed to get right, and trying to work out how he could get Nelson away from the wedding and to the game.

He wondered if he could somehow find a way of splitting up Nelson's sister and her fiancé, but he wasn't sure how to go about doing that, and it seemed rather harsh on the happy couple.

Then he spent a while trying to come up with a plan to get the hotel where they were holding the wedding shut down so the ceremony would have to be postponed. A local takeaway had been shut down a couple of months ago when they had an infestation of rats. He'd seen rats occasionally at the park - maybe he could catch one, release it at the hotel and call the council so it would be shut down too? But he wasn't sure how to catch a rat, and it would probably all take too long anyway.

Maybe Nelson could divorce his parents. He'd heard of some American kid doing that. But that would take ages, and anyway, Nelson was perfectly happy with his parents, so that was a rubbish idea.

Try as he might, he just couldn't think of a solution, and he still couldn't get to sleep either. He looked at the clock next to his bed. It was 3 o'clock in the morning already. It would be time to get up soon. He got up and went to the toilet, before sorting out his duvet and pillow and getting back into bed.

He must have woken his mum up, because she came into his room and sat down next to him on the side of his bed.

'What's up?' she asked him quietly, stroking a strand of hair away from his face.

'Can't sleep,' whispered Danny.

'I guessed that,' said Mum. 'Are you worried about the match tomorrow?'

'Yeah.'

'I know it's easier said than done, but I learned a long time ago that there's no point worrying about things you have no control over. There's nothing you can do about it. What will happen will happen.'

'That's just it though, I can do something...' He stopped himself. He'd almost told Mum all about it, and he wasn't sure he wanted to do that. As it happened though, he needn't have worried.

'This is about all that stuff you do on match days isn't it,' said Mum. 'Don't think I haven't noticed,' she continued when she saw the surprise on his face. 'Cheese rolls and pickled onion Monster Munch every single Saturday lunchtime, wearing the same football shirt to the match, even when it really should be in the wash. Some sort of routine you've got going is it?'

Danny nodded.

'Right, well, as long as you do the same again it'll all be fine, you'll have done all you can won't you?'

'It's not that easy though, Mum. Not tomorrow.'

'Oh right, because you need Nelson to do it too?'

He nodded again. There was no hiding anything from her was there?

'His sister's wedding isn't it? Well, that it is a big day for their family. You might just have to do it without him. It might still work mightn't it?'

'You don't understand. I tried it without him once before and it didn't work properly. I need him there tomorrow. Chadmouth Town needs him there.'

'Well, as I said, if you can't do anything about it, there's no point worrying about it.'

'He has to be there though.'

'Well, you'll just have to think of something then, but staying awake all night's not going to help you do that. Just relax, get some sleep and trust your subconscious.'

'My what?'

'Your subconscious. The brain's a funny thing. Sometimes it comes up with answers when you're not looking for them, like when you're in the shower, or on the toilet… or asleep.'

'Really?'

'Yeah. Happens to me all the time.'

Danny tried not to think about his Mum sitting on the toilet coming up with all sorts of brilliant ideas. Getting ideas while you were asleep sounded good though.

'Thanks, Mum.'

'No problem. Now, off to sleep.'

She kissed him on the forehead and made her way back to bed.

Danny was asleep within minutes.

Chapter 36

It was the morning of the match. THE match. Danny woke up at eight o'clock, feeling like he'd only had had a few hours sleep, probably because that's exactly what he'd had. His parents would have struggled to get him out of bed if it had been a school day, but today was different. It was Saturday, and he was anxious to get up and start getting ready, in the right way of course. Unfortunately, despite his late-night conversation with his mum, he hadn't woken up with a brilliant way to get Nelson away from the wedding and to the match, but he could at least make sure he did everything else right.

He jumped out of bed and opened the curtains. It was going to be a lovely, sunny day. Perfect, he thought, for defying the odds and avoiding relegation. He quickly got dressed, checking and double-checking that he was wearing all the right clothes, then ran downstairs for his Weetabix.

After he'd cleared up his breakfast things and cleaned his teeth, taking care not to dribble any toothpaste on his Chadmouth shirt that might prompt his dad to tell him to take it off and wash it, he realised he didn't have anything else to do. It was too early to do the luck dance, and he didn't have Nelson with him to do it with anyway, but he just couldn't concentrate when he tried to do anything to kill some time like watching videos online or reading. He kept looking at his phone to check the time. It was going much more slowly than usual, he was sure. The morning was really dragging.

Danny started going over everything in his head. He'd had the right breakfast and was wearing the right clothes, and he knew they had all the right things ready for lunch. He still had to come up with a way to get Nelson there though, and was Gran coming with them, and would that mean going a different way to the ground? There was so much that could still go wrong. Was he going to fail right at the end, just when he'd started to believe he could save Chadmouth from relegation? Dad had been right about having hope - it would hurt even more if they lost now.

He was still wondering whether Gran was going to go to the match or not when the doorbell rang. He ran to answer the door, half hoping it would be Nelson.

'Ooh, well that's a nice welcome isn't it?' said Gran with a smile when she saw the look of disappointment on her grandson's face.

'Sorry Gran,' said Danny, 'I thought it might be...'

'Nelson. I know,' she told him, stepping inside and taking her coat off. 'I'm sorry to disappoint you, but don't worry, I've decided it's best if I don't go to the match after all. I thought I'd come round here to listen on the radio, if your mum doesn't mind of course. That way I can see you before you go and when you get back. And we can celebrate together then can't we?'

Danny smiled. He really hoped they would be celebrating together later.

He followed Gran into the front room as she sat herself down and made herself at home.

'Gran's here,' he called to his parents.

'Now,' said Gran, 'have you found a way of getting your friend to go to the match after all? It might be crucial.'

Danny shook his head.

'Well, you'd better get on with it hadn't you,' she told him. 'It'll be time to go soon.'

'I know,' he said gloomily. He was running out of time.

He left Gran in the front room and went upstairs to go to the toilet. It was whilst he was mid-wee that the idea suddenly hit him, just like Mum had said it might. It wasn't perfect, but it was worth a try. It might just work.

He finished his wee, skipped washing his hands even though he knew what his parents would say about that, sprinted downstairs and pulled on his trainers as quickly as he could.

'I'm just off to get Nelson,' shouted Danny as he ran from the house.

'I thought you said he…' Dad started to reply as he came out of the front room, but by then Danny was already grabbing his bike from the shed.

Chapter 37

He jumped onto his bike and began pedalling as fast as he could, left onto Station Road, past the turnings for Hope Street and Church Street, then left onto Newport Way.

It didn't take him long to reach his destination – the Rumwell Hotel. The actual wedding service had finished, and there were lots of dressed-up, happy-looking people chatting and laughing outside, posing for photos with the bride and groom and waiting for the food and the party to begin.

Danny quickly scanned the crowd, desperately looking for his friend. Eventually, he caught a glimpse of him, looking uncomfortable in his new suit. Danny left his bike leaning against a lamp-post and hurried over to him.

'Danny!' said Nelson, looking surprised. 'What are you doing here?'

'I've got an idea,' answered Danny. 'Where's your dad?'

'He was over there just now,' said Nelson, looking back towards the entrance. 'He's not there now though. Hang on, there he is,' he added, spotting his father sharing a joke with some other men.

'Come on, we need to talk to him,' said Danny, setting off determinedly in the direction of Mr Blackwood, attracting a few funny looks from the wedding guests in his jeans and football shirt.

'If you're going to ask him if I can go, I've already tried,' protested Nelson. 'Loads of times.'

'There's something I've got to try,' said Danny. 'By the way, what did you have for breakfast?'

'Beans on toast of course. Just in case.'

'Perfect.'

They reached Mr Blackwood, who spotted his son and his friend and broke away from the group of men.

'Oh, hello Danny. I wasn't expecting to see you here,' he said in his broad Scouse accent.

'Hello, Mr Blackwood. Um, congratulations on your, on this… congratulations,' managed Danny, not sure what you were supposed to say to someone whose daughter has just got married.

'Okay, thank you, Danny,' said Nelson's dad. 'I don't think you came all this way just to say that though did you?'

'Well, no, you're right, I just wanted to…'

'You're going to ask me if Nelson can come to the football match with you, aren't you?'

'Well, yes, I…'

'The answer is still no I'm afraid.'

'But Mr Blackwood…'

'I'm sorry Danny. As I've told Nelson, many times, this is a very important day for our family. So I'm very sorry, but the answer is no.'

'Can't I just go for a bit?' asked Nelson. 'It's just the party bit now.'

'What do you think your mother would say if she knew I'd let you leave your sister's wedding to go and watch a football match?'

'But Dad…'

'She'd freak! As would your sister.'

Nelson gave Danny a look that said "I told you so", but Danny was just getting started. He'd been rehearsing what to say in his head as he cycled over.

'Mr Blackwood. Remember the Miracle of Istanbul…' began Danny.

'Ah, the greatest night of my life. Apart from when I met your mother of course, Nelson. Liverpool were 3-0 down in the Champions League final in Turkey against AC Milan, but came back to win on penalties to become champions of Europe for the fifth time...'

'Yes, you've told us about it, millions of times,' said Nelson, wondering why Danny had got his dad onto his favourite topic when they needed to be talking about Chadmouth's match that they were both about to miss if Danny didn't get a move on.

'Imagine if you hadn't been able to go,' continued Danny, 'because someone in your family was getting married.'

'Oh.'

'Ah, yes, oh,' agreed Nelson, now realising what Danny was doing.

'Imagine if you'd missed out on being there, on experiencing that one, incredible moment, something you'd never, ever get the chance to see again.'

'Hm, I see your point. But, you don't even support Chadmouth Town, Nelson. We support Liverpool.'

'Yes, but it's my best friend's team. I want to be there for him. Please, Dad, I'll only be gone a few hours, then I'll come straight back. The wedding will still be going on then. No one will miss me.'

Mr Blackwood looked thoughtful, then suddenly said, 'Bill Shankly!'

Danny and Nelson both looked blank.

'Bill who?'

'Bill Shankly. He said, "football's not a matter of life or death, it's *more* important than that".'

'Who's Bill Shankly?' asked Danny.

'Who's Bill Shankly? Who's Bill Shankly?! He's Liverpool's greatest ever manager, that's who he is. He started Liverpool on the road to greatness. Three league titles, two FA Cups, one UEFA Cup...'

'Yes, alright Dad, we get the picture.'

'My point is, son, Danny is right. You've got to go. This is more important than anything else to your mate right now, and if you're a good mate that makes it just as important to you. Go. Go now, while no one's looking. But come straight back. If your mum asks where you are I'll tell her I've just seen you but I don't know where you are now. She'll assume you're around here somewhere. Go.'

The boys raced off before he could change his mind.

'Thanks, Dad.'

'Thanks, Mr Blackwood.'

'And good luck!' he called after them, before adding under his breath as he shook his head, 'I'm going to be in so much trouble for this.'

He watched as Danny hopped back onto his bike, standing on the pedals as Nelson got on behind him for a backie. Danny began pedalling furiously again and they sped off back towards his house.

Time was running out. Would they have time to do everything they needed to do?

Chapter 38

They were back at Danny's house in no time. Danny dumped his bike on the front path and the two boys burst into the house.

'Your clothes are in my bedroom,' panted Danny as his mum came into the hall to see what all the commotion was.

'Hello Nelson,' she said. 'You look…'

Nelson raced straight past her and on upstairs.

'…smart.'

'Mum,' began Danny, still struggling to get his breath back. 'Can you get us a couple of cheese rolls with…'

'Pickled onion Monster Munch?' she interrupted with a smile on her face. 'Already waiting for you on the table. Lucky we had them in this week isn't it?'

'Brilliant,' said Danny, thinking that this was one thing that luck had not played in part in. 'Thanks, Mum. We've just got to quickly pop to the park.'

'Pop to the park?' said Dad, sticking his head out from the front room. 'You've not got time to pop to the park. What do you want to do that for?'

'We'll be mega quick, I promise,' Danny insisted, ignoring the question about why they wanted to go there.

'You'd better be. We can't be late, today of all days.'

Danny knew only too well how right his dad was, if he only knew it.

Just then Nelson came pounding down the stairs, having quickly changed into his t-shirt, jeans and trainers.

'Come on then,' he told Danny, and they sprinted out of the house, leaving Danny's parents shaking their heads.

Danny quickly grabbed the bag from the shed, Nelson jumped on the bike behind him again and they set off for the park.

'I hope no one else is there today,' shouted Danny over his shoulder.

'Who cares,' Nelson shouted back. 'What's the worst that can happen?'

There was nobody else at the park when they got there though, and they both grabbed their things and launched straight into the luck dance.

When they had finished they chucked their stuff back into the bag, got back on the bike and were back home in double-quick time.

'Don't forget to wash your hands,' called Dad as they plonked themselves down at the kitchen table and started tucking into their lunch.

Danny allowed himself a quick smile. So far so good. All they had to do now was get to their seats in the right way and it should all be fine. As long as the luck held that was. He tried to reassure himself that it would. That was easier said than done though. He hadn't had time to be nervous whilst he was rushing about all morning, but he was again now, and he didn't have much of an appetite, unlike Nelson who'd already scoffed his roll and was polishing off the last of his crisps. Danny managed to get it down him, just as Dad came in to check whether they were ready.

'Come on then you two,' he said. 'We need to go now or we'll be late.'

They picked up their plates to put in the dishwasher.

'Don't worry about those,' said Mum. 'You need to go. I'll sort them.'

'Thanks, Mum,' said Danny, letting her give him a kiss on his cheek.

'Good luck,' she said. 'Don't forget to see Gran before you go.'

Danny went into the front room when Gran was already set up in the armchair she always bagged when she came round, with a Chadmouth Town flag draped over the back and her Chadmouth Town scarf wrapped around her neck. She already had the radio on ready for the commentary to start, and looked as nervous as Danny felt.

'Is it all going to plan?' she asked him quietly.

'So far, so good,' Danny told her.

'Good. We'll be fine then,' she nodded, although she looked anything but confident.

'Danny!' called Dad from the hall.

'I've got to go,' said Danny, giving his Gran a big hug. 'See you later.'

'See you later love,' she said, before taking a big slurp of her tea.

Danny went and joined Dad and Nelson, and they headed down the garden path, around Danny's bike that he'd left in the middle of it.

'Right, I'm going to let you choose which way to go to the ground today,' his Dad told him. 'As if I couldn't guess.'

Danny was relieved to hear that, as it meant one less thing to worry about.

They were soon heading down Hope Street, turning left onto Harbour Road then right onto Short Street. Fans filled the approach to the ground, looking nervous and excited. The pub looked rammed, with people bringing their drinks out into the sunshine. It was clearly going to be packed in Springly Park today.

The three of them carried on towards the entrance of the ground.

'Three points today?' asked the programme seller as Dad handed over his cash to her, giving Danny a pointed look.

'Can't settle for anything less,' answered Dad, also giving Danny a look.

Danny just smiled. Everything was going according to plan.

'Going to the toilet Nelson?' asked Dad when they got inside the ground. He obviously knew they were up to something, but wasn't going to ask them what it was.

Nelson went off to the toilet, and Danny heaved a sigh of relief. He checked it all off in his head:

- Same clothes ✓
- Same breakfasts ✓
- Luck dance (done by both of them, properly) ✓
- Same lunch ✓
- Walk down Hope Street ✓
- Same conversation with programme seller ✓
- Only Nelson going the toilet ✓

They'd done all they could. Now Chadmouth just had to do their bit on the pitch. This was it – their whole season, and maybe their entire existence, had come down to the very last 90 minutes.

Chapter 39

Danny was expecting the Crabs to start the match nervously, but if they were nervous it didn't show. Within the first five minutes they'd had two good attempts on goal, a Ferguson snap-shot that the Beddingley keeper managed to tip around the post and a Logan free-kick that flew just over the bar. It was an encouraging start for the home supporters, and they were giving their team all the noisy support they could.

Chadmouth were trying to play a quick passing game but the big Beddingley players were just kicking their opponents if they couldn't get the ball. The referee was probably the busiest man on the pitch, as he blew his whistle time and again to give Chadmouth free-kicks. Beddingley were clever though, and they were careful not to commit fouls in dangerous areas.

The crowd was starting to get frustrated.

'Book him, ref!' shouted the man with no shirt when Wilson was dragged back as he tried to break down the touchline.

'Send him off!' yelled both the men behind them, agreeing with each other for once, when Sanchez was brought down from behind.

Then the biggest howl of protest yet went up from the crowd, as a Beddingley player won a free kick with an outrageous dive.

'He never touched him!' shouted Danny.

'You need your eyes tested ref!' bellowed the man with no shirt.

The free-kick came to nothing, but it had set the pattern for the next twenty minutes, with Beddingley players going to ground whenever a Chadmouth player challenged them for the ball. They were still conceding free-kicks of their own too whenever Chadmouth tried to attack, making the first half very stop-start, and incredibly frustrating for the home fans. The Beddingley fans in the away end didn't seem to mind though. Their team only needed a draw to survive.

As they moved into first-half stoppage time, Beddingley won a free-kick with another blatant dive, midway inside the Chadmouth half.

'Why can't the ref see that they're cheating?' wondered a very frustrated Danny.

A Beddingley player placed the ball for the free kick. Everyone was in the Chadmouth box now, jostling for position, apart from the Beddingley goalie. The Crabs really couldn't afford to go behind. Danny held his breath. He had a bad feeling about it. The free-kick was taken, crossed hard at head height into the box. A group of players all challenged for it as it flew towards them. Someone's hand went up, and the ball hit it, deflecting it past Mortensen and into the goal. The crowd waited for the ref to blow for handball, but incredibly he just signalled a goal.

'WHAT!!!???' screamed Danny, Nelson, Dad and almost everyone else in the ground.

The Chadmouth players were going crazy, shouting at the referee and the linesman, and the manager, Wedlock, was doing the same to the other linesman.

'No,' Danny groaned. 'He can't give that. That was a blatant handball.'

The ref *had* given it through, and he wasn't going to change his mind. He gave a yellow card to Osborne for protesting too much, and Wedlock shouted for his players to get on with the game, worried that someone might be sent off and they'd have to play the rest of the match a man down.

Boos rang out around Springly Park as the game restarted, and got even louder a few seconds later when the ref brought the half to an end, drowning out the cheers and chants of 'Going down, going down, going down!' from the Beddingley supporters.

Dad blew out his cheeks.

'Well, we're just going to have to do it the hard way,' he sighed.

'What is wrong with that ref?' asked Nelson.

'I don't know,' said Dad. 'He should have booked half of their team for fouls and the other half for diving, and how he missed that handball…' He shook his head.

'That could have just relegated us,' moaned Nelson.

'It's not over yet,' said Danny hopefully. He knew they'd done everything in their pre-match ritual right today, even if it had been a bit rushed. Surely their luck would still come good, even if it hadn't so far. 'I reckon it's going to be a game of two halves.'

'I hope you're right,' said Dad.

'It will be. It will be,' said Danny, trying to convince himself as much as the others.

Chapter 40

There was a cheer as the Chadmouth players came back onto the pitch, followed by more boos for the Beddingley team and even more for the referee.

'Don't upset the ref,' said Dad. 'We need him on *our* side in the second half.'

Danny smiled. He had a sneaky feeling he was going to be.

Chadmouth started the half a bit too enthusiastically, hitting a couple of long balls too hard, straight out for goal-kicks, but Wedlock shouted some instructions to them and they started to string some shorter passes together. Most of their attacks were still being ended by cynical fouls though, and the ref received an ironic cheer when he finally booked one of the offenders.

He was still being conned by the Beddingley players' dives though, until about ten minutes into the second half. One of the Beddingley midfielders went down theatrically after a perfectly good challenge by Parker. He looked up from the ground at the referee, expecting a free kick, but the ref waved play on. Chadmouth were on the break. Logan slipped the ball outside to Wilson, moments before he was taken out. Wilson took the ball deep into the Beddingley half and held it up, looking for options. Duffy made the overlap, and Wilson passed it for him to run on to. He took one touch, and without looking up crossed it into the box. His cross was inch-perfect, picking out Ferguson near the penalty spot, but the big striker's first touch wasn't great, and he wasn't able to shoot. Sanchez was arriving in the box though, and Ferguson teed him up, rolling the ball into his path. Sanchez shot. The ball skidded along the turf, past the despairing dive of the Beddingley goalie, and hit the post.

The crowd groaned, but the ball didn't rebound back onto the pitch, or out of play. Instead, it was rolling along the goal-line, gradually getting more and more over the line. Everyone in the ground knew that the ball had to be completely over the line for it to be a goal. The goalie, a defender and Ferguson were all racing towards the ball, desperate to get there first to either clear it or make sure it went in. The goalie won the race, and he dived onto the ball, flicking it away from the goal with his fingertips, and the defender booted it into touch. Ferguson turned and appealed to the ref.

'Was it over the line?' asked Nelson, looking anxious.

'I hope so, but I don't think so,' answered Dad. Danny thought he was right, but he was still hoping it would be given.

'This is huge,' said Danny.

The ref wasn't sure if the ball was over the line or not either. He trotted over to the linesman for a second opinion. The crowd watched them deep in conversation for what seemed like forever, until they saw him nod his head and start to walk away. He put his whistle in his mouth, gave a shrill blast, and signalled that it was a goal.

The crowd erupted, and Sanchez got booked for taking his shirt off to celebrate his goal. Danny and Nelson got covered in someone's drink that they'd thrown in the air in celebration at the equaliser, but they were too happy to mind.

'Maybe that ref's not so bad after all,' said Dad when they eventually sat back down.

Danny smiled to himself. It looked like their luck was in again after all, despite what had happened in the first half.

'Now we just have to find a winner from somewhere,' said Dad.

'We will,' said Danny. 'We will.'

Chapter 41

Chadmouth were now enjoying their best period of play of the match so far. Their smart passing was running rings around Beddingley, who weren't even getting close enough to kick them. They were peppering the Beddingley goal with long-range shots, winning corners and playing through-balls into the box that the visiting defenders were having to cut out with desperate, last-ditch challenges.

'A goal's coming,' said Nelson, picking up on Danny's belief.

'Don't jinx it,' Dad told him. He didn't look at all confident, but then, Danny thought, he didn't know that they'd done the luck dance and the rest of the routine perfectly like they did.

Time was ticking on though, and the second goal hadn't come yet. Danny checked the time on his phone. Fifteen minutes to go. Still time. It was getting unbearably tense though. Wedlock decided it was time to gamble, so he took off Parker and replaced him with Watson, an attacking move that gave the young academy player the chance to be a hero again. It seemed to make little difference though, and the youngster looked very anxious every time he got the ball.

Then, with ten minutes to go, disaster almost struck. With Chadmouth pushing more and more players forward in search of a winner, Beddingley won the ball in midfield and played it through towards their striker. He got to the ball first and lobbed it over Mortensen as he raced out of his goal. Everyone held their breath as the ball bounced, on towards the goal… and over the bar.

The crowd breathed again as the striker held his head in his hands.

'Oh my goodness, that was a let-off,' gasped Dad.

Danny and Nelson exchanged a glance. Their luck was holding, but they were running out of time.

A minute later it was Chadmouth on the attack again. Watson played a neat one-two with Logan on the edge of the box. He turned and shot in one movement. The ball flew through the air, curling as it went, heading for the top corner. The crowd got to their feet. Was this the moment? But no. The goalie got a fingertip to it and pushed it onto the post. It bounced back though, into the six-yard box, where Ferguson was waiting for it. He seemed unsure whether to kick it or head it. He chose to head it, ducking down to the ball as a defender tried to boot it away. He got there first, but his header flew agonisingly wide as he tumbled down in a heap with the defender.

The crowd groaned.

'I can't take much more of this,' said Dad, looking absolutely drained.

'Is he okay?' asked Danny, noticing that Ferguson had stayed down and that the physio was racing on to treat him.

'I think he got kicked in the head as he bent down,' said Nelson.

There was a moment's breather for everyone as Ferguson was treated.

'I hope the ref's stopped his watch,' said Dad.

Eventually, the physio helped Ferguson back onto his feet, but only to lead him slowly off the pitch. Fortunately, Chadmouth still had one substitution left, and Houchen quickly got his tracksuit off and prepared to come on. It was bad news though. Ferguson was their top scorer, and they needed a goal now more than ever.

For the first time since the match had started, Danny started to fear the worst. Had their luck finally run out? Were they going to fall just short? He ran through everything in his head for the hundredth time. He was sure they'd done everything right, but maybe he'd missed something. Perhaps they'd done something wrong. He couldn't think of anything, but he had a terrible feeling that they had. Had he accidentally put the wrong pants on? He wasn't going to check, but he was sure he hadn't. Had he missed something else though? Were they going down, and if they were, was it all his fault?

Chapter 42

The match restarted with a Beddingley goal kick, the ref being happy that the kick to Ferguson's head had been an accident. A ghostly quiet filled Springly Park now. Time was almost up, Chadmouth had just missed a good chance, and their top scorer had gone off injured. Nobody was leaving yet, but plenty of fans had just about given up. A few people were already in tears.

'Five minutes of injury time,' said Dad, spotting the fourth official's board.

'Only five?' said Nelson.

'That's enough,' said Danny, his confidence now coming back.

It was the lift the crowd needed, and they were suddenly sparked back into life for one final effort. They roared their team forward – 'Chadmouth! Chadmouth!' - knowing that one goal would be enough to keep them up. Everyone in the ground was on their feet now.

Chadmouth won a free-kick, just inside their own half. Everyone was sent up to the Beddingley box apart from Mortensen, who came out of his goal to take the free kick. He fired it into the Beddingley box. Watson was shoved to the ground. The crowd and the Chadmouth players screamed for a penalty... and it was given.

This was it. This was the moment they'd been waiting for. The chance to save their season. The tension was unbearable.

Captain Sanchez took responsibility himself.

'I wouldn't like to be taking that,' said Dad.

Half the crowd couldn't watch. Danny realised he was biting his nails. His heart was pounding like a heavy metal drum solo. Sanchez placed the ball on the spot. You could hear a pin drop. The ref blew his whistle, which echoed around the silent stadium. Sanchez started his run-up. He fired the ball at the goal. The goalie dived the right way though and got a hand to it. The crowd groaned, but the ball had dropped invitingly inside the six-yard box. Every single player tried to get there first. There was still a chance for the Crabs, but the goalie recovered first and dived onto the ball. Sanchez fell to the ground in despair, and had to be helped up by his teammates and told to keep going.

'That's it,' said Dad miserably. 'That was the chance.'

Danny didn't know what to think. He no longer knew whether he believed or not, whether they'd done everything right or not. It was too much to think about.

There was still time though, and the players hadn't given up yet. The crowd gathered itself for one more effort and roared as Osborne set off down the left-wing. A defender raced over to him and tried to scythe him down, but he saw the challenge coming and leapt over it. He kept on going, got to the byline, and fired in his cross. It was headed away, but behind for a corner.

'This is it. This is it,' said Danny.

'This must be our last chance,' said Nelson.

Everyone came up for the corner, even the goalie Mortensen. If Beddingley won the ball and broke quickly the Chadmouth goal was completely open, but it really didn't matter if they lost now. A draw was no good. They had to win.

Sanchez was closest to the ball, and he raced over to take the corner, desperate to make amends for his penalty miss with a great delivery. He signalled that he was ready to take it, ran up, and drilled the ball into the box. It looked too low though, the ball barely getting off the ground. Half a dozen players challenged for the ball, and it hit someone's foot and ballooned up into the air. Everyone watched as it fell back down as if in slow motion. Who would it fall to?

Down it came. It was falling just behind Mortensen. The big goalie watched the ball over his shoulder as it tumbled towards him. What was he going to do? All of a sudden, he jumped into the air. He angled his body, still keeping his eyes on the ball, and unleashed a powerful overhead kick at the goal. The ball flew, past everyone in the box. Only the Beddingley goalie could keep it out. He threw himself at the ball. He got a finger to, but it wasn't enough, and the ball, still travelling at speed, bulged the back of the net.

There was pandemonium. Mortensen, still lying on his back in the penalty area after his overhead kick, was buried under a pile of jubilant teammates, and the crowd was making more noise than Danny had heard in his entire life. Some fans had run onto the pitch to try to join in the celebrations but were chased and caught by the stewards. Danny, Nelson and Dad were jumping up and down, cheering, punching the air and hugging each other, as was everyone else. The Beddingley players looked distraught though, as did their supporters.

It took a good few minutes for the referee to restore order and for the game to restart, but no sooner had Beddingley kicked off than the ref blew for full time, and the celebrations really began. Now the stewards stood no chance keeping everyone off the pitch, and there was soon very little green grass to be seen as the ecstatic Crabs supporters poured from the stands, some waving their arms around madly, others with mobile phones out to record the incredible moment.

The fans lifted their heroes onto their shoulders, and everyone was cheering and singing 'We are staying up, we are staying up!' Danny, Nelson and Dad made their way down onto the hallowed turf to join in with a moment they would remember for the rest of their lives. Danny had never, *ever* felt so happy, and he doubted he ever would again. Chadmouth were staying up, and hopefully could put their money problems behind them too now. He wished Gran had been there to see it with them though, and he spared a thought for the Beddingley fans too, knowing exactly how much they would be hurting right now.

He wasn't going to let that stop him from celebrating though, and nor was anyone else. Some men had climbed up on top of the goalposts in which the famous goal had just been scored, and Danny was sure he recognised one of them.

'Isn't that...' he started to ask Nelson.

'Mr Quibley!' Nelson agreed with him, laughing his head off at the sight of their headteacher perched on the crossbar waving his Chadmouth scarf wildly above his head.

What a way to escape relegation. It almost made their rotten season seem worthwhile.

Chadmouth Town 2-1 Beddingley City
Kenton Athletic 3-3 Northford
Plumborough Town 2-2 Estonpark Borough
Stimport Rangers 0-1 Marshfield County
Timton United 0-0 Finbury Rovers

		Played	Won	Drawn	Lost	GD	Points
19	Finbury	46	12	9	25	-22	45
20	Chadmouth	46	9	14	23	-31	41
21	Beddingley	46	9	13	24	-20	40
22	Plumborough	46	7	16	23	-31	37
23	Kenton	46	7	15	24	-32	36
24	Marshfield	46	6	17	23	-35	35

Chapter 43

It took quite a while to get off the pitch and out of the ground. Nobody wanted to leave the scene of the most unforgettable football match they'd ever seen. It was a match that they'd remember forever, and they'd all probably be telling people about it for the rest of their lives, just like Nelson's dad did with the Miracle of Istanbul.

Nelson needed to get back to the wedding, even though he was enjoying himself immensely. He'd pretty much given up on getting back before his mother and sister noticed he was missing, but he still thought he should get back as soon as he could.

Danny and his dad would happily have stayed longer, celebrating with the other jubilant supporters, but they also wanted to go home to tell Gran all about it and to celebrate with her. They picked their way through the crowd inside the stadium and past the fans who were lining the streets outside, chanting and singing and enjoying a few drinks from the pub.

They could still hear the celebrations when they got to the junction of Station Road and Church Street, which Danny had been happy to walk down on the way home. Danny and Nelson carried on towards the hotel whilst Dad headed back home. Nelson had decided not to bother changing back into his suit, as he was sure his mum and sister would have worked out where he'd been.

The wedding reception was still in full flow when they got there, making almost, but not quite, as much noise as the Chadmouth fans had been.

'Do you want to come in for a bit?' asked Nelson. 'You're welcome if you want to.'

Danny was tempted by the delicious food smells coming from within the building. It was a long time since the hurriedly-eaten cheese rolls and pickled onion Monster Munch, but he needed to get home.

'I'd better not thanks. I need to go and see Gran. Enjoy the rest of the wedding though.'

'Thanks.'

'Will you get into trouble?'

'Probably not. Maybe. I don't know. It was worth it anyway,' he grinned. 'Thanks for taking me.'

'Thanks for coming,' said Danny. 'We couldn't have done it without you. Literally.'

'You might actually be right.'

'I'll see you on Monday then,'

'Yeah, see you on Monday.'

Danny turned away from his friend and started jogging back to his house.

When he got back he went straight into the front room to see his gran. She stood up from her chair and held both hands in the air in triumph, forgetting that she was holding a large glass of fizzy wine and slopping most of it all over the sofa.

'The Crabs are staying up, the Crabs are staying up!' she sang. Danny joined in.

'So now you gotta believe us, so now you gotta believe us!'

Mum and Dad came in to join them, carrying their own glasses of wine, and joined in too, even Mum, who wasn't even a football fan.

'So now you gotta believe us, the Crabs are staying up!'

'Feeling better then, Mum?' Dad asked Gran as she flopped back down into her chair.

'On top of the world,' said Gran.

'Promotion to the Championship next season I reckon,' said Danny.

'Steady on,' said Dad. 'We were seconds away from League Two an hour ago.'

'Let the boy dream,' Gran told him. Dad nodded with a smile, and he and Mum left them to it.

'So, tell me all about it, from kick-off to final whistle,' Gran told him.

'Weren't you listening to the commentary?' asked Danny.

'Of course, but it's not the same as hearing it from you.'

Danny took a seat on the sofa opposite her, took a deep breath, and told her all about it, reliving every minute with a huge grin on his face.

When he'd finished, and Gran had helped herself to another glass of wine, she sighed, and although she was smiling Danny thought she looked a bit sad.

'Do you wish you'd been there?' he asked.

'Of course I do,' she told him, 'but it was probably better that I wasn't. We may not be quite so amazingly happy right now if I had.'

'Do you believe it then? About me and Nelson and the luck dance, and the rest of our routine?'

She nodded thoughtfully.

'You know what, I think I do.'

'It is a shame you weren't there though.'

'I'd have loved to have been there, but we've got to do what's best for our team though, haven't we?'

'Yeah, we have.'

'Besides, there's always next season to look forward to isn't there. Do you really think we can get promotion?'

'Why not? If Nelson and me keep doing the luck dance before matches…'

'It won't work.'

Danny was stunned.

'What do you mean?'

'Your luck dance. It won't work next season.'

'But, it worked today, and for the last few games. Why can't it keep working?'

'I don't know, but it won't. You're incredibly lucky if you ever find something that actually works. Some fans try things they think will bring their team luck all their lives and never find anything that does. You and Nelson found one, but they never last. We were lucky it lasted until the end of the season. It certainly won't work across two seasons.'

'It might, you don't know that. I'm sure it'll even work when you start going to matches again, if that's what you're worried about.'

'Thanks, Danny, but it's not that. You remember I told you about my ritual, the liquorice rhyme that helped us win the FA Cup? Well, that didn't work the next season. We just had average luck. Nothing out of the ordinary. Not too good, not too bad.'

'This might be different.'

'Maybe, but don't get your hopes up.'

'Okay. We might get promoted anyway though.'

'Of course. There's always next season.'

'There's always next season.'

Gran smiled at her grandson and his eternal optimism. She knew it was exactly what you needed to support a small, lower division team.

'One thing is for sure Danny,' she told him. 'Whatever happens next season, you saved us this time round. You really are a super fan.'

Danny smiled back at her.

'Just call me Danny Mann - Super Fan.'

Did you know...

…that leaving a review for this book on Amazon will bring your favourite team lots of luck?

Well, it might or it might not (it probably won't), but it's worth a try isn't it? Seriously though, if you enjoyed this book I would be very grateful if you (or a grown up helper) could put a quick review up on Amazon. You don't have to say a lot - a line or two is plenty. As an independent author I'm not backed by any big publishing companies, and Amazon reviews are a really great way to show others that my books are worth a read.

Here's the link to review it on amazon.co.uk if you've got a spare minute.

THANKS!

Join my Readers Club

Another Chadmouth Town football story is on the way. To be the first to know about it and my other new books, and to receive sneak peeks you can join my Readers Club at ianslatter.com .

You can also find out about my new books by following me on Amazon, Goodreads or Bookbub.

Thanks for reading this

Ian

Coming soon

The Man With the Magic Foot – The second Chadmouth Town FC book.

I'll let you know when it's available if you (or a grown-up) join my Readers Club at ianslatter.com, or follow me on Amazon, Goodreads or Bookbub.

Have you read Eco Worrier?

What are you going to read next? Why not try my first book, Eco Worrier?

What readers have been saying about Eco Worrier:

- Five stars for a book that deserves it!
- This book is not only funny and awesome but it also teaches you a ton of interesting things about the planet.
- Kids will eat this story up and their parents will likely enjoy it too.
- A great story.
- Nicely-paced, imaginative and breezy tale which young teenagers (of all ages...) will enjoy.
- If you care about the environment, this is a book to give to your children.
- I highly recommend it for older kids and young adults.
- This was adorable! And super fun!
- It is incredibly readable, has big current issues and personal moral issues too in an entertaining and relatable way.
- An enlightening reading experience for young readers.

Here are the first few chapters for you to see if you fancy it:

I hate politics

'So anyway,' Marty continued, 'after that a pair of velociraptors wandered out of the toilets and into our classroom, licking their lips and burping because they'd just eaten Jamie Tancock, who'd just gone in for his one o-clock poo, but luckily we were saved by some aliens who all looked just like The Queen, who'd just landed on the cricket pitch, who kindly blew them up with their laser cannons. Of course, then we were all abducted and subjected to hours of torture on their spaceship, but they returned us all in time for home time.'

'Oh, that's good then,' said his mum, without her eyes leaving the TV.

Marty sighed. No one *ever* listened to a word he said. He was getting used to it now. When the Politics Channel was on at tea-time he really couldn't expect to get any sort of conversation out of either his mum or Emily, his little sister. His mum had an excuse he supposed, what with being the Prime Minister and all that, but Emily? What was her problem? She was an eleven-year-old girl. Why was she so interested in politics?

Everyone said she looked and sounded just like her mum, which she seemed to love. Fortunately, nobody had ever said that to Marty. Female, middle-aged, ever-so-slightly-frazzled politician – not a good look for a twelve-year-old boy. Emily was always saying she wanted to be Prime Minister too when she grew up, or *PM* as she insisted on calling it. He thought she probably would as well. She was definitely annoying enough.

On the TV a load of men and women in dreary, dark suits were sat in rows in the House of Commons, where Mum seemed to spend most of her time, listening to one bloke who was stood up, droning on about something or other. Mum was supposed to be there now, but she'd got delayed on the way back from a visit to some country or other, Marty couldn't even remember which one, so someone was standing in for her. From time to time the other MPs would either like what they heard or not like what they heard and would do a weird kind of mumbly shout to either agree or disagree with him. It was mind-numbingly boring.

'Can't we turn over now?' Marty begged, before shovelling another forkful of rubbery, microwaved lasagne into his mouth.

'No,' snapped Emily. 'We need to watch this. The Chancellor is giving a very important speech.'

Marty had no idea who this Chancellor person was, or what he was on about, and he didn't want to either. He seemed to be banging on about some airport that he thought should be built, and if it wasn't built it would be very bad news, in his opinion. To be honest though, he sounded like the sort of person that if he told you you'd just won the lottery you'd end up thinking something terrible had happened, like a fatberg had blocked up the sewers and your house had ended up six-foot deep in raw sewage.

Marty didn't know who he was, but he had seen him around, arriving for meetings there at 10 Downing Street. The caption at the bottom of the screen said he was called Sir Jarvis Skelton, and he had a posh voice to match his posh name. He looked posh too, but there was something creepy about him as well.

'Which is exactly why I think we should turn over to something more interesting,' Marty argued. 'I think there's international paint drying on the other side, or maybe a repeat of a classic episode of celebrity grass growing.'

'Why don't you go and watch the paint in your bedroom if you're such a fan?' Emily told him.

'Why don't you go and…'

'That's enough you two,' interrupted Mum. 'Can't you both just get along for once? I do want to watch this. I should really have gone straight there from the airport. I'm sorry Marty, but once it's finished maybe we can see what else is on then.'

'When this has finished you'll be going back to work and Emily's off to her meeting so I'll be on my own again and I can watch whatever I want.'

'Ooh, what will it be, Marty Farty, paint drying or grass growing?' sneered Emily.

'Oh shut up,' he told her. 'And don't call me that.'

'Both of you shut up!' snapped Mum. 'I can't hear a word he's saying now anyway. Why can't you both just enjoy the nice meal and try to be civil to each other for five minutes? For goodness sake, it's like being in a Cabinet meeting trying to keep control of you two.'

Marty and Emily both fell silent. He wondered if Mum was able to control her fellow MPs like that. He did wonder about pointing out that calling three microwaved lasagnes and a few bits of limp lettuce a "nice meal" was pushing it a bit, but he didn't think that would go down too well just then. Just like the lasagne wasn't going down too well, as Mum had somehow managed to overcook it. She was definitely a better politician than she was a cook. It was pretty rare for the three of them to be eating tea together too, not that any of them were making the most of their quality family time.

If you were thinking for one moment that it sounded pretty cool, living in one of the most famous houses in the country, you'd be very wrong. It was dull. Dull, dull, dull. As dull as watching the Politics Channel 24/7 - unbelievably dull. The constant stream of boring, stuffy politicians and advisors who came to the house (which is the Prime Minister's office as well as her home) the endless security checks whenever anyone went in or out... it was all so tedious. If Marty wanted to just go to the shops, go for a burger or go out skateboarding, it all had to be planned in advance and cleared with security, and if he did go anywhere he had to have a security guard with him at all times. He kind of got why, but that didn't stop it from being a right pain in the bum.

Not that Marty had any friends to go anywhere with anyway. He used to have some great mates back where they used to live, but he didn't like any of the other kids at the posh school he'd had to transfer to when they'd moved from their old home to London, and they didn't like him either. Put it this way, if your idea of fun was agonising over whether to go to Oxford like your mum or Cambridge like your dad, or boasting about how much your birthday party cost, or casually mentioning which celebrity happened to be on your family's yacht at the weekend, you'd probably have fitted in really well. It wasn't Marty's, so he didn't.

Emily seemed to like it at Number 10 though. She loved politics as much as Mum and thought living in the heart of British government was great. She'd wanted to follow in Mum's footsteps for as long as Marty could remember, and living where she did, seeing and hearing what she did, was the best education she could possibly get, as she said *all* the time.

Marty sometimes wondered whether he should take more of an interest in what Mum was doing, as Emily did. She always knew exactly what was going on, what was at stake, but he just couldn't be bothered with it all.

On the TV someone seemed to be disagreeing with the Chancellor bloke now, talking about climate change, getting more mumbly shouts and causing other MPs to get up to demand their say.

'How do you think it's going to go Mum?' asked Emily.

'I really don't know,' Mum answered. 'Some MPs are convinced that the airport needs to be built and others are just as sure that it shouldn't because of climate change. What do you think?'

'I'm not sure either. I'm sure Parliament will make the right decision though.'

Marty pulled a face. What a creep. He didn't give his opinion, partly because he didn't have one and partly because no one would care if he did. He was all for everyone doing everything they could to stop climate change of course, but he didn't really know anything about this airport, and he didn't want to either. He could have done without it being forced down his throat on the telly too, although, to be honest, it was a slight improvement on the lasagne.

The debate *finally* came to an end, and some woman with a microphone was now stood on the lawn outside the Houses of Parliament, explaining just how important it all was.

'Can we turn over now then?' Marty pleaded.

'We're still watching this,' answered Emily.

'But Mum said we could turn over when the speech finished.'

'Let's just see what the analysts have to say about it first, then we'll turn over.'

'Why would anyone care what anybody has to say about it?'

'Why would anyone care what *you* have to say about anything?'

He'd had enough. He grabbed the remote control off the table and pointed it at the TV, but before he could change the channel Emily snatched it off him.

'Give it back!' he yelled at her, trying to grab it back, but she held it out of his reach and laughed.

He grabbed her arm and her laugh turned into a screech.

'Marty! Get off her now!' shouted Mum, plucking the remote control away from both of them.

Now he'd definitely had enough.

'It's not fair!' he yelled. 'You always take *her* side. It's always about what you two want, never about what I want! You never listen to anything I say!'

'Marty…' started Mum, but he was already off and was running out of the room.

'I hate politics, I hate this house and I hate you two!'

'Marty!' she called after him, but he ignored her as he stomped back to his bedroom. He slammed the door behind him and hurled himself down onto his bed, fighting back tears of rage.

The gorilla-wrestler

Marty lay there, face down, for a few minutes. He half wondered if Mum would come after him, but he knew that she wouldn't. She was needed at some *hugely important* meeting back at the House of Commons after tea, and of course, she couldn't keep *them* waiting, could she? Emily was going out to her Young Politicians meeting as well, so it was just him in the house this evening. Well, and the security staff.

Oh, and Larry the cat, who he hadn't noticed was sat on his windowsill, who'd probably been fast asleep until he'd made his dramatic entrance. Larry jumped down, then up onto the bed.

'It's alright for you,' Marty told him, tickling him between the ears. 'You get to come and go as you want. You even get the policemen outside the front door ringing the doorbell for you, don't you?'

He wasn't really their cat. He belonged to the house. Prime Ministers and their families came and went, but Larry stayed there. He even had an official title - Chief Mouser to the Cabinet Office. He seemed to know it was his house and everyone else was just a guest, although that's pretty much what all cats think about their houses. Marty liked Larry, and he was glad Mum had insisted on living in Number 10 rather than Number 11, like most Prime Ministers with kids did. Next door had bigger bedrooms, but it didn't have Larry.

He turned over onto his back, turned his TV on and channel-hopped for a while. There was literally nothing on though. He thought about going on his phone or laptop, but he wasn't in the mood. He just needed something different to do.

He looked around his room for ideas. The one good thing about being the son of the Prime Minister was the gifts that you got from all sorts of world leaders and celebrities who visited Number 10. In the last year, since his mum became PM, he'd been given all sorts of things, from a space helmet by a Hollywood film director to a life-size inflatable crocodile (no, he had no idea either) by some ageing rock-star he'd never heard of but who was apparently a big supporter of Mum's party.

He'd even been given a set of pens by the head of Britain's secret service, a nice old man who looked as unlike a spy as you could possibly imagine. Emily got one too and seemed delighted, but Marty hadn't been too impressed at first, until the man told him that one pen was a mega-powerful torch and the other was a state-of-the-art listening device. He suggested Marty could use them to 'have some fun with his friends'. Marty asked him if he could also have a sports car with a range of rocket launchers, tyre-cutting blades and a smoke-screen device, but the man just chuckled and told him they were out of those.

The worst present he'd been given was a signed book about how great the US President was, written by the US President, given to him by the US President. Marty hadn't liked him much, and he certainly hadn't read his book.

He let out a giant sigh. Tomorrow was the first day of the summer holidays, which meant he had another six weeks of boredom to deal with. He used to love the summer holidays, before they moved there and he had to switch to his new school. Back when he used to have friends and was allowed out of the house to see them. He really missed them.

Marty was fed up with being in his room, and in the stupid house. It was all so unfair. He hadn't asked for his mum to get elected Prime Minister. He hadn't asked to move there and become a virtual prisoner. He felt like he just had to get out of there. He jumped up and stormed out of his room, down one floor to where all the meeting rooms were, and downstairs again. On the stairs there were photos and paintings of every British Prime Minister there'd ever been, like a kind of selfie gallery, without the pouts or peace-signs of course.

'Boring old farts', Marty told them as he stomped past them, 'the lot of you.'

He was tempted to give them glasses and beards, fangs and sticky-out tongues, to make them a bit more interesting, but he didn't have a pen with him, and anyway, he didn't have time right then – he was leaving.

He ran over to the front door and tried to open it, but it was locked. He yanked at the doorknob, and hammered on it with his fists as hard as he could.

'Let me out! Let me out!' he yelled furiously.

It didn't take long for someone to come and see what was going on. He heard the sound of footsteps thudding across the floor, and a shadow filled the hallway. The huge body of Leishman, Number 10's Head of Security, skidded to a halt next to him. The rumour was that he wrestled gorillas in his spare time, two at a time, although to be honest, why London Zoo would let him wrestle one, let alone two of their gorillas Marty wasn't sure. He looked like he could have though, if they let him – he must have been nearly seven feet tall, and almost as wide, and no-one had any idea how his uniform didn't split under the strain of his gigantic muscles. He fixed Marty with the scowl that he permanently wore, his wild eyes boring into him, and a low growl emerged from deep within his fearsome, ginger beard.

More security guards arrived seconds later, not quite as big as Leishman, but all looking ready to tackle a major security alert. They looked a little disappointed to see that it was just the Prime Minister's slightly weedy (if he was honest) son. Marty wasn't in the mood to be intimidated by any of them though.

'Let-Me-Out-Now!' he demanded.

'I can't do that,' Leishman told him calmly, shaking his head. His voice had surprised Marty the first time he'd heard him speak. He sounded, well, normal. He'd expected him to have a giant voice to match his giant body, but he didn't.

'It's alright,' he told his colleagues. 'I've got this.'

They returned to wherever they'd been, and whatever they'd been doing, excitement over. He put his hand gently on Marty's arm to guide him away from the door, but Marty angrily shook it off.

'I'm going out,' he insisted.

'No can do. It's not been cleared with your mum.'

'You can't keep me locked up here.'

'It's for your own safety.'

'Yeah, right.'

'What do you think would happen if you stepped outside of that door anyway? You wouldn't be able to get past the security at the end of the street. And even if you did, we can't just let the son of the Prime Minister wander in and out as he pleases, can we? You'd be hassled by the press and probably kidnapped by terrorists within seconds.'

'Really?'

'Definitely. Well, definitely the first bit, possibly the second bit. But it's not a risk we can take now, is it?'

Marty sighed. Leishman had a point, he supposed. It was still depressing being stuck in that prison though.

Leishman seemed to have had enough of talking in the hallway.

'Come on,' he said. 'Let's get you away from here.'

He put a hand firmly on Marty's back and ushered him towards the lift. Yes, they had a lift in their house. It was cool at first, but the novelty wore off pretty quickly. They stopped on the first floor, and Leishman led the way towards the Cabinet Office. It was the most important room in the building, where the Government had its meetings and basically ran the country.

It was also the most private. What was Leishman planning to do to him?

A way out?

Inside the Cabinet Office was quiet and calm. There was a portrait of someone important-looking above the fireplace and a huge, oval-shaped table in the middle of the room, already laid out for the next meeting with pads of paper, pens, glasses and big water jugs. You could feel the history and importance of the room. Everything looked old and important, from the chandelier hanging from the ceiling to the heavy curtains drawn across the huge windows at the back of the room, keeping the sun out and the room cool.

Leishman pulled a chair out from the table with a meaty hand and slowly lowered himself onto it. Despite being careful it still creaked under his bulk. Marty stayed where he was, wondering why they were in there. Did Leishman have some punishment in mind for him to make sure he didn't try to escape again? The security guard could tell Marty was nervous.

'Don't worry, I don't eat people,' he said. 'I might rip their arms off, or tie their legs together, or stick their feet in their ears. Never eat them though. Not any more anyway. Not since I became vegan.'

Marty thought he was probably joking, so managed a small, nervous laugh. He wasn't entirely sure though.

'It's Marty isn't it.'

It wasn't a question, but Marty nodded an answer anyway.

'Well Marty, how do you like living at Number 10?'

'Boring. Totally boring.'

'Yeah, I can see that this isn't the most exciting place for a twelve-year-old boy. You are twelve aren't you?'

'Yeah, it was my birthday last month.'

'Ah yes, I remember now. I had to keep an eye on your party. Your Mum invited all the kids of her fellow MPs around to the house, got a string quartet in to provide the music and the Downing Street chef prepared a selection of gourmet canapés.'

'Ugh, don't remind me', Marty grumbled. 'Worst birthday party ever.' They both shuddered together at the memory. Marty pulled out the chair next to Leishman and sat down.

'So, Marty,' said Leishman, trying to change the subject. 'Now you've had a look around the Cabinet Office, what do you think?'

'It's alright,' said Marty.

'Alright? Alright?! This is probably the most famous office in the country. One of the most important in the world. Just think of all the historic decisions that have been made by the country's greatest political minds over the years – Walpole, Pitt the Elder and Pitt the Younger, Disraeli, Gladstone, Lloyd-George…'

He noticed Marty's blank look.

'No? None of them?'

Marty shook his head.

'The Duke of Portland? The Earl of Shelburne? Don't tell me you've never heard of The Marquess of Rockingham?'

He kept on shaking his head.

'Jeez. What do they teach you in school these days?'

'Are they the old farts on the stairs? They look totally boring.'

'I guess you've got a point there. Politics is pretty boring if I'm honest.'

'So is this house.'

'Hm, I wouldn't be so sure about that,' Leishman said mysteriously. Marty waited for him to tell him more, but instead he said, 'You know, it might be a bit boring in here too, but it is nice and quiet. If you ever want somewhere to do your homework, feel free. As long as there's no-one else in here of course.'

'Isn't it usually locked?' he asked.

'Nope. No need. We check it first thing every morning but after that, anyone can come and go as they please, once they're inside Number 10 of course.'

'Okay, well, I might do that. I have got some projects to do over the summer holidays. That's about as much excitement as I'm going to get I suppose. As I'm not even allowed to go outside.'

Leishman thought about this for a while, then leant in closer. He glanced around him before speaking.

'You know,' he said in a low voice, 'I shouldn't be telling you this, but, would a secret passage out of Number 10 be of interest to you at all?'

'A secret passage?' repeated Marty, matching his whisper, wondering again whether to believe him or not.

'A secret passage,' he repeated, waggling one eyebrow in a way that he probably thought was full of mystery. 'Of course, I couldn't possibly confirm or deny that it exists, but let's just say, if I was you, and I was going to look for it, I think there's a very strong possibility that I would find it, if you see what I mean.'

Marty nodded, even though he didn't.

'I think I might find myself looking for a hidden floor underneath the building, only accessible via the lift.'

'Via the lift?' Marty repeated, louder than Leishman wanted, and the big man looked around anxiously again. Marty lowered his voice back down. 'Wait, what, there's a button in the lift marked "Hidden Floor" or "Secret Passage" or something is there?'

Leishman glanced round for a third time.

'No. Of course there's no button marked "Hidden Floor" or "Secret Passage". It would hardly be a secret then would it?' he tutted. 'No, you have to press *Number 10*. I mean, that's what I might try, if I was looking for it, you know.'

'Number 10? I don't remember there being a button with a 10 on it. And there aren't ten floors. Wouldn't people keep pressing it to see where it goes?'

Leishman just leant away and hauled himself to his feet. He gave Marty a theatrical wink, then strode towards the door.

'So, how are you supposed to press Number 10 if there isn't a Number 10 button?' Marty called after him.

Leishman paused at the door.

'That's something I'd have to work out isn't it,' he said, opening the door, 'if I was looking for it. Which of course, I'm not. Because I haven't actually confirmed that it exists. Have I?'

He frowned, as if he was trying to work out whether he had or not. Marty was glad it wasn't just him who was confused.

'Maybe it does, maybe it doesn't. Then again,' he added with another, even more theatrical wink, 'maybe the world's your *oyster*'. He left the room and closed the door behind him.

Marty stayed in his seat, thinking about what he'd just been told. Was Leishman joking about a secret passage? Surely he was. Marty thought he seemed the sort to enjoy a wind-up. He'd probably keep a lookout for him trying to work out how to make the lift go down to the secret floor, then come along and have a good laugh. Then again, he thought, he couldn't see him as the sort to try to humiliate a twelve-year-old kid. Maybe he just thought it was a good story.

He'd had enough of the Cabinet Office for one day, so he said 'see you later' to the man in the portrait above the fireplace, opened the door and headed back to his room.

He couldn't help wondering though, was there really a secret passage?

TO KEEP READING, SEARCH FOR **ECO WORRIER**

OR **IAN SLATTER** ON AMAZON OR SCAN THIS QR CODE: